Toothdecay

and Other Stories

By

Shells Walter

ISBN: 978-1-7329136-9-1

TABLE OF CONTENTS

Grown

The road started to look never ending. It would only be a few more miles before Karen and Russ were at their new farmhouse. Karen sighed. It was her idea to move away from the city to give the girls a better environment. She still wasn't sure she had made a good decision.

The radio played the local country station and dust came though the window from the road. Russ turned to look at Karen, patted her on her arm and turned to focus on the road. There were very few cars that drove by and there was only farmland for miles separated by more crops. The old, broken down, wooden farmhouse on their right, was theirs. Russ turned, drove up the gravel driveway and stopped in front of their newly bought home.

"It'll be okay," Russ said and turned to Karen, placing his hand in hers. Karen smiled briefly, opened the truck door and stepped onto the gravel.

Russ opened the truck door, stepped down and looked at the house. It was beaten up for sure, wooden boards falling half down, paint chipped and the window shutters barely hanging on. He smiled anyways. It was going to be a project he was looking forward to. He stepped over some of the pieces of wood from the door and walked inside.

Inside the house, the condition was not much better. The cupboards were a pale yellow; most of the paint had worn off. There was a beaten up stove on the side that looked like it had not been replaced since the 1950's. He turned when he heard a sigh come from Karen.

"Are you sure this is a good idea? I mean what if we can't find a decent school for the girls or maybe they won't like it here?" She pleaded with her eyes, waiting for some reassurance from him. He walked over to her grabbed her shoulders and gently nudged her into his arms.

"Honey, everything will be fine. I know it will. The girls are with their grandmother for a few days and I'm sure she is spoiling them rotten. It will give us a few days to get the house somewhat in order before they get here." He smiled as he held her closer to him.

"I guess you're right. It's just that at times I wonder if pulling us all out of where we were at because I felt uncomfortable isn't being selfish."

"Maybe a little." He giggled and she pushed away from him, gently hitting him on the shoulder with her hand. He grinned and looked around some more. A few things here and there and he knew this place would be perfect for them.

***

The next day started early for Russ. Neither he nor Karen had slept well on the old mattress that became their bed for the evening. He crawled unwillingly off the mattress, almost rolling off, stretched, yawned and walked out to the kitchen. Karen had gotten up before him and was making coffee. The smell reminded Russ of being back in Milwaukee.

He came behind her, wrapping his arms around her waist kissing her gently on the back of her neck. She turned to face him, holding the coffee pot in her hand.

"What's on your agenda for today?" She asked and poured some coffee into the mugs she had put on the old wooden table.

"I was thinking of going downtown and see what the hardware store has to offer. I'm hoping to get some things done here to fix up this place." She smiled and sat down across from him.

"So, what are we doing about those fields out there?" she said and took a sip of her coffee. "They seem to be empty with nothing in them." Russ turned to look out the back window. The fields had not been kept up for a long time and he was trying to think of what crop to plant in them.

"I have no idea what to do with them; maybe an idea will come up when I go down to the hardware store. Some of the local farmers might be able to help me think of an idea."

"Are you sure they will be friendly?" Karen joked.

"Well, it won't hurt to try." Russ got up, put his mug in the kitchen sink and went to get dressed. A short time later, he was dressed in a plaid shirt, shorts and a baseball cap that was bought a long time ago when he saw his first game in Milwaukee.

"Okay, I'm off," he said and walked up to Karen who was still sitting by the table, kissed her quickly and headed out the door to his new red pick up truck.

The roads were smoother than he had thought they would be heading toward the downtown area. He pulled up to the corner, parked his truck, got out and looked around. There were only a few buildings that made up the downtown business area. The shops were basic need types for the town. The pharmacy had the only neon lights in the business district which reflected onto his truck in a white hue.

The hardware store was on his right and he headed over to it. The sign read, *Central Hardware Store*. It was basic and to the point. Above the door was a bell that rung as he opened it and walked inside. An elderly man, in his seventies, stood behind the counter organizing some papers. The man looked up briefly at Russ and then went back to what he was doing.

Russ walked down the aisle that was labeled paint. Red paint is what he thought he should paint the barn and house, cliché he knew, but he liked it anyways. He studied the different types of paint when he heard footsteps behind him. Russ turned to see the old man that had been behind the counter staring at him.

"Bill, here," the man reached out his hand, Russ shook it. "You're new here?" The man asked and Russ nodded.

"Looking for paint? We have some of the best here." Bill took a paint can from the top shelf and handed it to Russ. Russ took the can and looked at it.

"Just trying to get the barn up and going you know," he said as he looked at the paint can, and then set it back on the shelf.

"You bought the James's old farmhouse a few miles up the road?" He asked Russ who had already moved on to the next can of paint and was studying it.

"Uh, yeah, up the road," he said and made a decision that was the can of paint he wanted. He started walking back to the counter, Bill followed him.

"Started crops yet?" Bill asked as he rung up the sale of the paint.

"Uh, not yet, I'm not even sure what I want to plant." Russ reached into his short's pocket for his wallet, pulled out some cash and set it on the counter.

"I think I have an idea for you, that's if you're interested," Bill said.

"What would that be?" Russ asked as he took the receipt and stuffed it into his pocket.

"We have a farmer's meeting here every Tuesday, next one is tomorrow night at eight sharp in the evening. You're welcome to join us, could help with your problems."

Russ looked at Bill for a moment, grabbed the paint can and walked toward the door to go out. He turned for a moment.

"I'll think about it, thanks," he said and Bill nodded.

Russ opened his truck door, plopped the paint can on the passenger seat, hopped in and started driving the car back to the farmhouse.

He turned on the radio which produced another country station. A horrible smell rose from the air through the window as he drove. Russ turned to look out his window briefly to try and see where the smell was coming from. His nose squinted in disgust. He turned back to focus on the road, but the smell became unbearable. Once again he turned to look out his window; this time he caught a glimpse of a couple of men that looked like farmers, pushing something into the dirt in one of their fields.

His mouth stayed open as he stared at the sight of the two men. Shaking his head, he turned back to looking at the road. His mind was not able to place the thought of seeing two men pushing what seemed like human arms into the ground. Russ smiled and assumed it was because he was tired from the move down here still.

The truck moved slowly up the gravel driveway and stopped. Russ got out, grabbing the paint can as he did and looked ahead at his open fields. A slight shimmer of something bright caught his attention. He walked closer to the start of the field and stared. The light became brighter. Russ bent down, moved some of the grass and weeds out of the way and saw what looked like a finger. Quickly, he stood back up and almost fell backwards.

"What the hell?" He screamed out. Russ stood there in shock. The door to the farmhouse swung open and Karen came running out.

"What's wrong?" She ran over to Russ who was frozen in fear. He just pointed to where he saw what he thought was a finger.

"Honey, what? I don't see anything, what is it?" Karen got more concerned as she watched her husband. She walked over to where he was pointing, but she saw nothing. Karen stood back up and turned to face her husband, grabbing his arm.

"Russ, what is it, what did you see?" She saw his eyes widen.

"I, I don't know. There was something there." Sweat dripped down his forehead and Karen took the paint can from him, set it down on the grass and gestured for him to sit down on the picnic bench that faced the fields.

"Honey, are you okay, you have me worried now," she said in a softer tone. He nodded, trying to reassure her.

"It must be because I'm tired," he said, trying to make her feel better, but he didn't believe what he was telling her. There was something there. He saw it. Why it was there or if he saw the actual finger, he wasn't sure. The image still strong in his mind and he shook a bit.

"Russ, why don't you come inside and rest for a bit, lay down or something. When you wake up I'll have lunch ready, maybe you're just tired and hungry." Karen got up, took his hand and led him back into the house.

Russ followed willingly. If by chance she was right that he was tired and hungry, a nap wouldn't hurt him.

***

The hardware store closed at five in the evening every night. Bill locked the door and went back to the counter. His friend Jerry was still in the backroom, but came out after closing.

"I heard you talking to that new guy," he said to Bill who was putting keys away in a cabinet facing the back wall behind the counter.

"Yeah, thinking he make a great addition to the farmer's community," Bill said, turning around looking at Jerry.

"Hope so, last ones weren't that great, crops looking bad this season. We need something." Bill nodded.

"I think it will be good. He seems willing to make an effort here."

"Good, cause we need that," Jerry replied, grabbing his coat and heading out the door of the hardware store.

***

Russ woke up from his nap. It was already evening out. He got up from the mattress and walked over to the window that faced the crops, lights shown on the crops, leaving a shadow on the picnic table. He walked closer to the window, looked out and stared. Something poked out of one area of the crop in plain view. Russ opened and closed his eyes repeatedly to focus more clearly at what he was seeing.

A decayed human arm waved gently in the small breeze. Russ felt goose bumps forming on his arms and a cold feeling ran through his body. Yet curiosity filled his blood and he walked through the house out the back door. He moved slowly toward the arm, not sure if something would happen if he got closer to it. As he approached the arm, he saw shadows out of the corner of his eye and he stopped.

Two men stood by the edge of the crop opening. Russ stood still as he looked at the men.

"What are you doing here?" He asked. His voice still shaken by what he saw.

"Oh, Russ, we like to help the new farmers out by looking at their lands. We meant no intrusion." Bill turned to Jerry who had a grin on his face. Jerry extended his hand but Russ did not take it.

"I'm Jerry It's nice to meet you. I'm part of the farmer's group that Bill talked to you about." Russ didn't say anything. He turned back to look at the arm that was still swinging back and forth in the wind.

"Oh, Russ, don't worry about that. It helps our crops to grow," Bill said. Russ turned quickly to look at Bill.

"What?" He yelled.

"The bodies help to make our crops grow better. Karen didn't tell you?" Bill looked over at Jerry who stifled a laugh. Russ ran away from both of them into the house.

"Karen?" He yelled through the house, but he couldn't find her. Russ stood in the hallway, sweat dripping down past his arms to the floor. His breath became labored and he wondered where Karen had gone, what the men outside just said and if he could get out of this house as quickly as possible.

He ran to the front door but Karen blocked it.

"Karen?" He was startled and stood just before her.

"Honey, I'm sorry. I knew you wouldn't come here if I told you the truth. Do you forgive me?" She cocked her head sideways, giving a desperate look in her eyes. Russ was shaken. He had no idea what to do next. If Karen, like they said, knew about all this, what did it mean?

"I…" Russ was not able to finish his sentence before he heard footsteps behind him. About a dozen men had gathered in the front way to the door, led by Bill and Jerry.

"Hi ya Russ, these are a few more farmers from the group. They wanted to welcome you and say hello." Bill grinned. Russ turned back to Karen who also was now smiling.

"Karen?"

"Russ, it has to be this way. These people are my family, my real family. The crops were bad. The last ones didn't work out as good."

"The last ones?" Russ asked, not sure if he wanted the answer.

"The last family that was brought here." She looked at him. Her eyes were not as sweet as he remembered.

"That what, that who, who was brought here and by whom?" He asked.

"Well, by me of course Russ. You didn't think you were my first did you?"

Russ's mouth dropped open.

"The girls, what about the girls?" He pleaded with her to give him the answers he needed.

"They're not yours."

"But, but I saw you give birth. I saw you…"

"That you did, but they were never yours. It was all part of the plan to eventually get you out here. It took a bit longer to get pregnant again, longer than I had hoped." Her eyes darted back and forth to Bill, then to Russ.

Russ looked down at the floor. His thoughts ran about like a tornado. He tried to think clearly. It had been going on for years and he had no idea. His mind was not able to wrap around everything that was going on. Russ's instinct kicked into gear and he made a run for it. He looked quickly at his gold watch noting the time. If he got out of the house soon, he could make the plane ride, get out of here and never be a part of it again.

He pushed past the men who stood watching him run out the back door to the crop area, running as fast as he could, but suddenly tripping over the paint can that was never picked up from earlier in the day. Russ groaned in pain from his newly acquired sprained ankle. He managed to move his leg and got up. He turned quickly for a moment to see if they had followed him. The last thing he saw was a shovel coming right for his head.

***

"I think this is going to be good for us," Jim said driving his truck down the old road.

"I know it will," his wife replied.

"It will help with the stress you have been feeling. You needed a break from the city." Jim grabbed her hand and squeezed it.

"Thanks you're the best."

They kept driving down the road. The woman looked out the side of her window. She saw the crops had bloomed. The house they had just bought was approaching in their view. She smiled as she saw the crops to the right. In the faintness of her view, an arm waved gently in the breeze. A bright shimmering light was caught by the sun. A watch still told the time that it stopped two years before.

"Karen, it will be a lot of work, but I think we can do it." Jim smiled.

"I know we can honey, lots of work, but well worth it in the end." She smiled at him, turned away from the crop and they both walked into their new farmhouse.

And They All Fall Down

Gray ashes fell from the sky. Jeremy looked up; another day of the industries burning the dead. It had been like this since 2010 when the cloning of people became law because of the plague. The Government's solution: clone the surviving people to find a cure.

Jeremy looked back down at his feet that were sore from walking with the worn out leather shoes. It had been months since the plague had started. People were acting crazy and Jeremy wanted out of the city. Papers were no longer publishing, broadcasts on television no longer airing, Jeremy had no idea how far the plague had spread. He did know that he would do anything to find Bobbie and his daughter, Jessica.

Bobbi and Jessica disappeared a week after the plague had started. Jeremy had been away on a work trip across the city. He couldn't get back to his house. The lines were down so no way to even use his cell. When Jeremy was finally able to get back, Bobbi and Jessica were no longer there. He took only the things necessary with him and started out into the city.

Jeremy arched his back. The aches and pains he experienced were spreading throughout his body. He had been walking for about a month, back and forth through out the city. His body was now telling him to rest. He sat down on the curb that stood in front of what used to be his favorite book store. The bookstore, along with other businesses, were burnt to the ground; destroyed by looters or the Government.

The only true buildings that remained were the cloning establishments and research departments. There were several across the border of the city. Police guarded the border with protective masks. There were only a few now. The plague had spread to them as well. Infected people had tried to cross the border in hopes they would find a salvation on the other side.

Jeremy looked down the broken road on his left. He had already traveled down it several times and no sign of Jessica or Bobbi. A few people at the building next to him scurried in to try to find any remaining food left in the abandoned restaurant. He watched in sadness as others fought one another for a scrap of bread that was on the ground.

This was how it was now; people fighting to eat and just fighting to survive. Jeremy shivered as he watched one man bash another's head in with a baseball bat. The man then ran with the stolen bread crust. The plague did this to people; made them fear, made them animals.

Jeremy stood up. His hands still shook. If he turned to the right he could get away from the people fighting and maybe, just maybe, find something he didn't see before.

"Food over here!" A man screamed as he ran past Jeremy. Jeremy glanced as the man ran into another woman already fighting someone for a piece of rotten fruit. He moved slowly away from the group and started walking down the road.

Jeremy adjusted his homemade mask. It had taken him awhile, but he had finally gotten the sheet just aligned correctly with his face. He hoped that it would protect him long enough from the plague so he could find Jessica and Bobbi. Two men walked past him. One of the two started coughing. Jeremy made his way quickly to the other side. Once the cough starts, the rest of the airborne virus takes hold. A few days later you die.

Jeremy shook his head. Milwaukee used to be such a great city. There was always something to do and so many people to do it with. Now ruins of the night life were scattered through out the streets. If there were people on the road, it was those who dared to find food, or try to find a way out of the infected city. The air wasn't polluted by industry plants anymore, but by a virus that spread as quickly as wild fire.

He kept walking down the road. The sun beat down hard on Jeremy. He wiped away beads of sweat forming on his forehead. A building marked with a large three stood on his right. It was one of the cloning facilities. A large metal door provided the entrance into this secret atmosphere.

Jeremy looked around. He often wondered about these places when they were built. What actually went on behind this metal door? Two lights, one red, one green, told when the door was locked and when it could be opened. He stared at the door, and then turned to see if anyone was around him. Staring at the lights, he tried to figure a way to trick them into thinking he had the right code to get in. Jeremy tried to remember the simple codes people always made a mistake in using; the ones that became easy to trace and easy to hack into.

He sighed as he remembered his job as a tester. It seemed so long ago that he used to get paid to see if he could hack into sites to test security settings. Jeremy studied the number pad located on the right side of the two lights. It was a set of ten numbers: zero through nine. His fingers now dried out and chapped, played around with the digits on the pad. After a few tries, he looked and saw the green light come on. A smile crept across his face.

The metal door swung open slowly. A long corridor awaited Jeremy as he walked inside. The door shut hard behind him. He walked down an endless display of lights flickering over head. Jeremy squinted his eyes, focusing on some lettering that was on a door up ahead.

CLONING PHASE 1

The window showed two scientists in typical white jackets. Jeremy watched from a distance as the two men picked apart a human who had died from the virus; their skin was a light blue hue, a sign of the virus, oxygen depravation. Jeremy's eyes scanned over to the other table. There was another body with a plastic sheet covering it.

"That's got to be the clone," Jeremy whispered to himself. He stepped backwards away from the window and crushed his foot on a piece of metal. The two men in the room turned to see where the noise came from.

Jeremy noticed the two men coming closer to the window to look. He turned quickly around the corner and waited. The knob turned slowly and the two men came out of the room.

"I know I heard something," one of the two men said. The other man turned and looked down the left corridor. Jeremy just waited, hoping they wouldn't find him.

The two men crept along the side of the corner where Jeremy stood.

"Hey, what are you doing here?" One of the men asked. Jeremy, startled, ran down the side entrance. The two men chased him.

Jeremy turned to look behind him only once and saw the men approaching fast. He finally made it to the front metal door he came into. The number pads pushed with ease and he made it outside of the building. The two men stood by the front metal door watching Jeremy run.

Jeremy finally stopped down the road by the old school; his breathing heavy from the run.

He held his hands on his knees as he bent over to catch his breath. A young girl, about the age of his daughter approached.

"Mister, are you okay?" She asked. Jeremy stood up and looked at her.

The girl's brown hair was braided on top of her head and small earrings dangled from her tiny ears. Her concern was sweet.

"What's your name?" He asked her.

"Emily," she replied. Her feet shuffled in the old dirt that used to be the school's play yard.

"Hi Emily, I'm Jeremy." Jeremy studied her dress.

The girl's dress had been torn on the bottom, dirt covered the several layers. It had looked as if she had been out on her own for awhile.

"Mister, you shouldn't be out here now. People come looking for food, sometimes they are real nasty."

He watched as she turned one way to look down the road, then the other.

"Yes, I've seen that." Jeremy sighed. The girl was so young.

"People look different. My mom and dad, I don't know where they are." She kept looking around as if pleading that the world would give her back her parents.

Jeremy turned to look back at the cloning building, then back at Emily. He aligned his mask back up around his nose.

"Why do you have that on your face?" Emily asked. Jeremy looked at her confused.

"Do you know why these people look funny?" He asked her.

"No, I don't know. My mom and dad are gone. I came home from school, they were gone." Her voice started to shake. She looked back and forth.

"Emily, these people are ill." Jeremy looked at the young girl, hoping she would understand.

"Ill?" Her eyes squinted.

"Yes, ill. They're very sick. It's very catching. That's why I wear this." Jeremy pointed to his mask. Emily looked at the white sheet Jeremy had cut to form to his face.

"Do I need one of those?" She asked. Jeremy nodded.

"It would probably be a good idea." Jeremy looked around trying to find something that he could give her to use.

"I don't have anything like that." Her eyes pleaded with him.

"Well, we will have to look for something." Jeremy tried to make his voice as soothing as possible. He could see Emily was scared.

Emily nodded and followed Jeremy around the school to where the front doors used to be. Now only a gaping hole remained. They walked inside. Jeremy looked around.

"Do you remember where you went in here if you were sick?" He asked Emily as they kept walking down the old school hallway.

"It used to be down here," Emily replied, pointing to the right. They both walked down the hallway, rooms were on either side and the lights dimmed ever so slightly.

They finally approached a large room. Emily walked in.

"This looks like where it was," she said and Jeremy followed.

Inside the room there were tore sheets, beds over turn and a medicine cabinet that was bashed in from people stealing from it. The blue paint was chipped on the ceiling and pieces of it were on the floor. Jeremy looked around. It was amazing that the room was used for anything at one time.

"There's a sheet over here." Jeremy picked the tore sheet off the side of a bed that was turned over. Pulled at it to where it was a smaller piece, enough to put over Emily's face and looked for something to hold it on. He found a strip of Velcro in the drawer.

He placed the sheet over her face and the strip of Velcro around the back. Jeremy had managed to make two holes in the sheet, allowing the Velcro to be snug. Emily turned around to look at Jeremy.

"This will work?" She asked.

"It should for now. I don't believe I have gotten ill yet." Jeremy looked around the room once more. The window was cracked in the center. People didn't care about front doors anymore.

Emily walked out of the room. Jeremy turned and followed. They looked at each other, both wearing their masks. Jeremy sighed. When he moved to Milwaukee he had no idea it would end up being like this. His family, he still didn't know where they were. Then there was Emily who was with him now. How was he going to take care of her?

They walked down the hallway back to the opening of the school. The sun had gone down which was a bad time for this type of situation the city was experiencing. Jeremy held onto Emily's hand tightly. The night air was chilly.

"I'm hungry," Emily said looking up at Jeremy. Jeremy looked down at her.

"Um, well, we can see what we can find," he replied. Emily looked down. He knew a young girl shouldn't have to experience this kind of ordeal.

They walked out onto the road. Jeremy constantly looked back and forth waiting to see who would come after them. In the bushes along side one of the old buildings, a man sat waiting. He was hungry and cold; anything would work for him now to stay alive. The man darted out at them. Emily screamed.

"I'm cold and your clothes will do fine," the half-naked man said to Jeremy. He lunged at him.

Jeremy pushed Emily out of the way. She fell on the dirt next to what used to be a grocery store. The man's strength was more than Jeremy's at this time. Jeremy fell to the ground with the man hitting his face. Emily kept screaming and watched as the man ripped off Jeremy's shirt, pushed him back down and put the shirt on.

Jeremy's mask started to show red patches. The man had broken a tooth and cut his lip. The man laughed and buttoned up Jeremy's shirt. Jeremy looked at the blurry image that stood over him. He wasn't sure in his daze, but he thought the man had the starting of the virus; the light blue coloring.

"Emily," Jeremy whispered. "Get away from him."

The man turned to look at Emily. Emily stopped screaming and stood up frozen where she was. The man smiled at her, turned and walked away from the two. Emily ran over to Jeremy.

"You okay?" She asked, kneeling down beside him on the ground.

"I think so," Jeremy whispered. He stood up slowly.

Jeremy looked around. His sight was a little less blurry. The man had left. He felt a chill coming on. His shirt had kept him warm during these horrendous nights. Emily stood staring at him.

"We should try to find some shelter for the night." Jeremy took her hand

They walked down the road slowly. Jeremy shook every so often from the cold. His mouth still ached where the man had hit him. He turned as he heard a siren; something only heard if it was a cloning vehicle. Jeremy ran over to the side building with Emily.

"You need to be quiet okay?" He whispered to her. Emily nodded.

The siren came closer. A white small, boxed looking car approached. A light scanned the area.

"What are they doing?" Emily said quietly.

"They're looking for the ill."

"Why?"

Jeremy looked at Emily. How was he going to explain they were looking for the ill to clone them?

"Um, well, they look for the ill to try and um, help them." He turned away from her staring at the car.

"Then why are we hiding?" She asked. He turned back. It was getting more difficult dealing with a child during this.

"Um, well, sometimes those people, um, can be harmful to people like us." It sounded good to him.

"But why us?"

"Because we're not ill." Jeremy looked at Emily who was very confused.

The car sped up. The light was still scanning the streets and bushes as it went by. Jeremy stepped out from behind the building. Emily followed.

"Let's go." Jeremy looked at Emily who nodded.

They started walking down the road again. The streets were littered with the rubble of the buildings, torn clothes and bits of ash left from the morning incineration of the dead. As they walked, Jeremy looked into some of the buildings. He saw a few people in the old clock store.

"Can we go in there?" Emily asked.

"No, we better stay by ourselves." Jeremy looked at her and grabbed her hand again.

"But why?"

"Because we don't wish to get ill." He looked back at the road ahead. A lot of the buildings were torn down completely. It would be hard for them to find anything to stay the night in.

"Are there a lot of people ill?" Emily's question surprised Jeremy.

"Yes, I'm not sure how many, but a lot," he replied.

"Are we going to die?" Her eyes showed tears forming.

"No." Jeremy wasn't sure of his answer, but he didn't want to worry her anymore. It was hard enough for a child during this time.

A building to their right showed even more people inside. It was the café Jeremy used to frequent on his lunch breaks. They walked by as they heard coughing. He grabbed Emily's hand tighter and walked faster by the five or so people located inside. The street lamp on their left flickered for a brief moment and then went out. Another siren roared ahead.

Jeremy turned quickly to spot the white car headed for them. He looked around for any place for them to hide. All the buildings that surrounded them now were either torn down or occupied by others. Jeremy started to panic. The car approached them and stopped.

"You two, over here," the voice from the loudspeaker said. Jeremy and Emily stopped walking.

"Now," the voice continued.

"What do we do?" Emily asked scared. Jeremy looked at her and then back at the car.

"Um, just stay here." Jeremy walked over to the car.

"You are supposed to come when called," the man in car said to Jeremy.

"Yes, but there is no law saying I should," Jeremy replied.

"You know we are trying to help you people," the man sounded agitated.

"What do you want me to do? Leave the child alone though," Jeremy pleaded.

"We can't do that. Everyone who vaguely seems not infected also has to come in for testing to see why they're not."

"Not the child please, she's so young." Jeremy turned to look at Emily who stood in the same spot where she was instructed.

"No, we need you both," the man replied and then gestured to another man in the back who came out to get them both.

The man went for Emily first and Jeremy ran over to her. The man pushed him out of the way and he fell to the ground.

"No!" Jeremy yelled after the man who held Emily. Emily turned to look at Jeremy, tears running down her face.

The man shoved her into the car, locked her in and came back for Jeremy. Jeremy got up and started to run. The man ran after him. Another building opening was up ahead. Jeremy ran into it. The man followed.

"You must come in," the man called after Jeremy. Jeremy just turned to look at him and turned back to see a bunch of people gathered around a homemade fire. They scattered as soon as the man in the white approached.

Jeremy kept running into the darkness. He fell over some rocks. One of them hit his head. Jeremy was knocked out.

***

Jeremy woke up dazed. The white lights showed a shadow in the room.

"Ah, good, you're awake," one of the scientists said.

"What?" Jeremy asked confused. The scientist ignored his question.

"You've been tested and we find some odd things about you." He turned away from Jeremy, picked up his chart and scanned it.

"Uh?" Jeremy tried to stretch his neck to see what the scientist was looking at.

"It seems here that you're a carrier of this virus, but only a carrier."

Jeremy looked at him confused.

"Through the DNA testing we have discovered that your daughter was also here."

"Daughter?" Jeremy asked, his family, here?

"Yes, daughter, they were killed by the virus and…"

Jeremy didn't listen anymore. The word 'killed' kept repeating in his mind.

"What we have done is taken your DNA and cloned you."

Jeremy looked over to the side. Another table stood with a plastic sheet over it. Inside the sheet was an outline of a man; one that looked just like Jeremy.

"What will happen now is we will provide more tests on this clone. A cure maybe in the near future."

"Cure?" Jeremy asked.

"Yes, a cure."

"What happened to the girl I was with?'

"She was killed."

"What?" Jeremy didn't want anything to have happened to her. He started to feel guilty that she came along.

"Don't be like that. It wasn't the virus." The scientists almost sounded sincere.

"I don't, what do you mean?"

"She was a clone that escaped here."

"Clone?"

"Yes, In fact she was a clone of your daughter. It was lucky for us she found you. It allowed us to get to her faster and bring her back."

"But why, what has she done to deserve that?" Jeremy's voice rose.

"She was infected with the full blown virus. Any contact with her was automatic death in a few days. You would have been dead anyways, but for some reason you have adapted into just being a carrier."

Jeremy was shocked. He knew now there was no way out of this. His family was dead. They were going to keep cloning.

"And me, what happens to me?" Jeremy dared to ask.

"You will be laid to rest."

"What?" Jeremy's eyes widened.

"You will be incinerated as we have no use for you anymore. The clone will provide everything we need to find a cure."

"But…" That was the last word Jeremy said.

***

"The United States is full of the virus. People are dying everywhere. Scientists all over Europe are working around the clock to provide a solution to the possible incoming disaster. The virus is thought to have been carried over by birds migrating from the US.

Specialists in the UK are considering using the same method of cloning as the US did to find a cure."

The television blared in the Smith's home of the outbreak. A cough was heard in the backroom where their daughter played.

Full of Yuletide Stuffing

Sara looked at the cut on her finger; she had missed the skin she was tearing up by an inch and took the tip off her own finger with the knife. Cursing for such a stupid mistake, she got back up off her blue wooden chair and walked over to the woman. If it wasn't for her, Sara would have been finished with this year's dolls. The woman's skin was too thick, making it harder for Sara to cut it off the body. It made her frustrated.

Her eyes narrowed as she kneeled down beside the woman's body, taking the knife and starting to dig it into the skin. Once again, the knife dragged slowly across the flesh. It caught in a section of the skin. Sara pulled the knife out and threw it down on the floor. She looked at this year's starting of her gifts. Women lined up against the wall, ready for cutting, preparing the skin, sewing and then placing it on the plastic mannequin. She would do the final details of the face make-up after the mannequin was fully dressed, so to speak.

The mannequin was a great touch. She had gotten the idea while walking through the mall and looking at the perfect figures. The women that Sara made to dolls just didn't have the most wonderful figures. The mannequins gave them what they never had. She shook her head at this woman. If she wasn't such a pain to cut her skin. She was a pain at work as well. Sara should have expected it would also be a problem to make her into a doll after she was dead.

Chris or Chrissie, as other co-workers had called her, had made Sara's life a living hell. She had lied to Sara's boss not only to get ahead in her job, but to ruin Sara's chances as well. It wasn't a hard choice for Sara to make a special doll out of Chrissie. Her own doll that no matter what the price offered, she would never sell. The other dolls ordered and paid for. Sara would have to have them ready soon and then her messenger would pick them up and deliver them. She was just about to pick up the knife and try cutting Chrissie's skin again when she heard the beeping of her cell phone.

She walked over to her phone and flipped open the cover. A text message alert appeared. She pressed a button and the envelope opened revealing the message.

I have an order for you. Please contact me at 555-6734.

Sara closed the phone. The orders started piling in a few years ago. It was amazing what people with money would or could pay for. She memorized the number and then took the battery out of the phone. There were never two calls to the same number. Sara made sure to use disposable phones. She didn't want anyone to stop her from making her dolls.

***

John honked the horn at the little Volkswagen Bug in front of him. He hated Christmas Eve traffic. His bakery van skidded across the wet road as he rushed to his destination. The deliveries and pick-ups needed to be tonight. If he didn't, the Sara woman wouldn't give him his money and he needed all the money he could get with gambling debts piling up. He had to find a way to make-up the money before his wife found out.

John never knew what were in the heavy bags. He never asked, just transported them back and forth to the addresses the woman gave him. John looked at the clock in his van.

"Shit," he said aloud. He knew he was about ten minutes late. The last time he was a few minutes late, he was docked a few hundred from his pay.

Pushing on the accelerator pedal harder, his van raced down the street. A dark blue house was up ahead. John pulled behind the house as instructed.

"Finally," Sara replied, irritated.

"I'm sorry, there was traffic and…" John fumbled around with his words.

"No excuses, now let me see what you have." Sara walked to the back of the van and waited.

John opened the van's doors and there laying on the floor stacked one by one in dark plastic bags, were the bodies Sara needed. John of course didn't know what they were and Sara wanted to keep it that way.

"Help me bring them inside," Sara said as she reached for the end of one of the bags. John nodded, went inside the van and pushed one of the bodies towards Sara.

They grabbed the first bag together and started walking up the back stairs to the house.

"Just place it here." Sara gestured to the floor right in front of the door.

"Wait here. I'll need help with the other two as well, but I'll get your money. As you know you will be docked at least a hundred for the delay."

John nodded and expected it. He watched Sara walk into the next room and then at the bag below his feet. Gently, he kicked at the bag. Whatever was in there was hard, but soft at the same time. His eyes narrowed, curiosity was growing inside of him. Maybe if he just would remove a corner of the bag he could see inside. John bent down to touch the bag when Sara walked back.

"What are you doing?" She demanded.

"I, well, I was just…" John stood back up.

"I told you no questions. You get paid pretty well for just picking up and dropping off."

"I just, well, Ms. I have been doing this for a few years now, don't you think it's time I knew what the cargo was I was shipping back and forth?" John shifted his feet.

Sara frowned. The man was now too curious for her. It was the perfect set-up. Why now did he want to know? She pretended to ignore him and walked outside. John followed her.

"Help me with these other two and you'll get your pay. Then this working relationship will come to a close." Sara walked towards the door, stepping over the body and down the stairs. John followed her.

"But, listen, I'm sorry I asked. I need this job. I need the money."

"No, you broke the agreement that is not something I tolerate." Sara walked to the back of the van and grabbed a hold of the next bag.

John climbed into the back of the van to help with the next bag. Sara grabbed too tightly to the plastic and tore a hole in the bottom. John leaned over to look. His eyes widened.

"Is that, is that a hand?" John stared at the hole of the bag and saw fingers of a human hand. "Is this what you have been asking me to...?"

Sara looked up from the bag. "Didn't I say no questions?"

John didn't reply but stood crouched in the van unsure of what to do next. Sara glared at him. Then, he turned around as quickly as he could to get his cell phone that was on the passenger's seat. Sara lunged at his back with the knife she had gotten when she went to get his money, something she had always done, but never figured she would have to use. The knife went in hard at first and then easily the rest of the way into John's back. He gasped, falling forward, blood now spilling down his shirt draining from the wound.

Sara watched him try to get his arm around his back to pull it out, but he couldn't make it. Soon, he stopped trying and died right in his van. She sighed, now she would have to move the bodies out herself and most of the time they were heavy. Smiling, she was happy that she lived close to the city, but not so close that she couldn't keep her dolls from pesky neighbors. Looking over John, she had decided that he wouldn't make such a bad doll and she was sure there would be someone requesting a male doll soon. Sara grinned.

***

Sara looked at her completed dolls all lined up against her wall, treated with rock salt, tanned and placed on the mannequins just so. Christmas had become her favorite time of the year. She loved giving the gifts of her dolls to people. They were always so generous in the compliments.

To think it all started with Daddy. He taught me the way.

Sara remembered how her father one Christmas day had given her a doll. The doll was well stuffed and so hard that it made it difficult for Sara to hug, but she loved that doll. She remembered when her father would kill those people in the basement and then stuff them as if they were animals in a museum. Sara had no idea at the time she would learn her father's trade and become one of the most requested doll makers in the world. All it took was a greedy mortician to help with the killing of the people and a few people her father knew to get the word around. The requests for her dolls came in the hundreds and always for Christmas day. It seemed that everyone wanted to make sure they had the perfect gift.

She took the gift tags out of the package and started to write on each one. Sara placed them one by one on a finger of the mannequin. She smiled. The dolls looked beautiful. There was now a new pick-up person one of her father's friends had suggested and they would be here soon to deliver her dolls. She went back to her chair and sat down. There would be more requests for dolls and more to deliver next year on Christmas day. She looked at one doll. The mannequin's hair was messed up.

Sara stood up and walked over to the doll. She frowned as she saw the brown hair dipping off the head to the side. Fixing it, she then stood back and took a good look at the doll.

"Perfect," she said out loud.

The male doll was ready to go out as a present to a client's mistress. Sara never asked what the dolls she made were for, but this client felt the need to tell her. It was nice that she already had the perfect mannequin for the client and John made a perfect doll. She knew it would be just what the client asked for. Sara grinned and made an x through this year's Christmas day.

I Smelled It

I <u>smelled</u> it. It was burning my stomach more than the rotting flesh that used to be my intestines. In the corner a woman waited for me. The cowering action of her movements made her smell more distinctive. I wanted her flesh. The hunger was excruciating.

I watched as the others made their way through the destroyed city. It would only be a matter of time before they smelled the woman. I moved closer to the woman. Her eyes darted back and forth in fear of something like me. I waited and watched her; then made my move as quickly as the rotting parts of me left could manage.

"No, please no!" Her scream enticed me more. I grabbed her arm.

At first she tried to pull her arm away. I just grabbed harder. It was then that the light in her eyes died and she went limp. She didn't die, but passed out due to fear. It worked for me. I was able to move her arm to my mouth with ease.

The flesh, <u>her</u> flesh, tasted sweet, tasted like distant memories of other women before I became what I am now. Oh the life was so grand back then, but it's not so bad now. I still get to do what I did when I was human; if you wanted to call me human. I'm not walking with many limbs in tact now, but I taste the flesh like I used to.

She squirmed when she regained consciousness. Her voice was no longer functioning, probably out of fear. My teeth were enjoying the bits of her skin getting stuck in the small crevices. Her blood oozed down my throat. I gnawed the rest of the way through her arm hitting bone. The bone snapped under my firm grasp.

I stopped biting and spit the bone fragments out. The bones I lacked interest in and didn't give me the satisfaction as the flesh. The woman had lost a lot of blood during my feeding frenzy. She fell back against the cement column of the old grocery store. I shoved her over to the side where no one could see her, my hunger taken care of for now.

I watched blurry figures chase a man down the road leaving a trail of their body parts as they climbed over each other to get to their prey. My vision was not as it used to be with one eye left. A short while later, a group of humans came. Their military vehicles roared down the broken road, shouting and gun fire along side. Competition for humans was fierce amongst my kind; humans trying to get rid of us, even worse.

I tried to focus on the other street off to the right. The trees blocked some of my view. I knew one of these days they would catch me, put a bullet in my head like they did the others. Finding a way to escape was something I was used to, even when I was human. Times were a bit different and I was different now, at least physically. Escaping a human's grasp became challenging.

When I was human things were so enjoyable. I could move about without care. Killing was something I enjoyed as much as living. I learned to escape and be hidden, taking care of the women and finding a place of solitude. Then as if punishment for my crimes, a virus came, just one person takes a combination of DNA, producing the end of the world. Me? I was one of the first to get bit, by one of my victims in the early stages. I had assumed when I was taking my knife to slit her throat that she was just another prostitute with some disease. I was wrong. Now I've become something that moves slow, that disturbs my way of doing things.

I turned to look at the woman again; her face now pale. She was dying. Even in the condition I was in, I felt a sense of greatness. I had killed again. The woman had deserved it. I was once again free of my hunger, my need to destroy the creatures that have destroyed this Earth. Perhaps the others just strived to fill their need. I did that too, but I had my other reasons. Those women needed to die.

As I turned back to the main road, I wondered if the detective that was after me when I was human was amongst the crowd of the living or one of my kind. It was hard back then to avoid him, but I did. Now? Now I don't know if I'm even a twinkle in his eyes. And if I was would he even recognize me?

It didn't matter now as I needed to move away from this area. The military had broken through the gates into this city, devouring all of my kind with a simple firing of one of their guns. It would be hard enough to get past them. I didn't need to think about what old detective Henry was doing. The woman would have to stay here. I wouldn't be able to carry her and move fast, what fast was considered for me now.

Moving across the grassy area was a bit rough for me; my legs dragging as if they were behind me instead of barely attached to my body. I heard shouting nearby and knew the humans were close. If I didn't rush this I would be the next dead thing on the ground.

I looked around at the buildings now present. They were not the same as I remembered so long ago. People were not the same. Technology still advanced with even a small amount of humans on the Earth. My kind advanced too. We were thinking creatures that fooled humans. The humans thought we were dumb and just grunted. We allowed them to believe that. It helped us to sneak up on them better.

Vehicles that now had something called wheels on them, military that drove even bigger things with guns that could hold several others. It was a disturbing site but one I got used to over time. The one advantage is these vehicles were very loud, alerting me to their coming, and I needed all the help I could get.

My kind didn't talk a lot to each other. Some of that was because we didn't have many limbs left, some because they wanted to be left alone in their own personal hell. It was all fine by me. I always have worked alone, better that way. There was no one who could tell me what I couldn't do, well, they tried. As one of these creatures it seems the most I can do is get by, especially since I'm so selective on what I chose to eat. It seems ridiculous, but that's who I was and am now even in this state.

I finally made it through the grassy area. I sniffed around for any humans, but there was none, safe for the time being. A house stood a few feet away. It looked like an old wooden shack. I looked at my clothes, a worn and torn coat from so many years of use, my pants that used to be black, and my shirt that use to be white, but now was black with blood spots. It amazed me they were still hanging on my body. As a human I was so much cleaner than this.

The door of the house had no lock on it so I shoved my shoulder against it. It flew open with ease. Inside the house was a few bowls filled with water, a towel, table and chairs. It looked like an old bath house, perhaps for servants or even rent for those vile women that worked at night.

I walked inside and shut the door. It would be soon that I would need to feed again and finding women of that nature was becoming easier. Every human was struggling to live and eat. Women were selling themselves in trade for food or water, even shelter. It was easy for me to spot these women. I could smell them. Their fear was even more desirable as I heard them scream.

I waited patiently. I assumed I was one of the few of my kind who did. Listening to the noise outside, I only hoped they would pass soon. The firing and the vehicles became louder. I knew it wasn't possible they had any idea I was in here. And if they did I would for the first time experience fear.

"You over there, now!" One of the men shouted.

I could hear the sounds of more of my kind coming and the shots being fired killing them. If I still had breath I would be holding it now, waiting and anticipating when those humans would fly through the door. I went to one of the corners of the room trying to see outside the small window in the house. My one eye strained to look through the murky glass. I only saw faint figures moving around the house.

"Anyone in here?" One of the men said. He pounded on the door.

I remained as quite as I could. He could have a gun. I didn't want my ending to be in this horrible house. The door creaked open. The man walked in and looked around. I was hidden in a dark corner and out of view of the man. He moved closer to where I was. I noticed he had no gun. He would be out of my taste group, but walking around still was something I valued more.

I took his arm.

"No!" The man yelled as he noticed I was there.

I couldn't reply to him, but could smell his fear. I moved his arm into my teeth that barely stayed in my mouth. The flesh tasted different and not to my liking.

The smell of his fear made it more interesting. I ripped apart his flesh on his arm and swallowed that piece whole. He screamed more.

I gnawed most of his arm down to the bone and took it with my hand, ripping it out of the man's socket. The man became limp after that. I had my hunger met for the time being and just let the man fall down to the floor. The relief coursed through my body, allowing me to try and venture outside of the house.

I moved around the man and pushed open the door. The noises had died down. I looked around. The images were a bit blurry, but I knew I could get past any humans still around. Then the smell came again. A woman standing by a tree smoking, puffs of smoke coming out of her cigarette. She was waiting.

I waited by the tree looking to see if any more humans were around her. There was no one. If I could smile still there would have been a huge one creeping across my face at the sight of this woman. Now, I just have the smell that drives me to move closer to her.

She didn't see me approaching her, didn't even know I was this close to her. If I could I would've laughed on how easy this was. I dragged my right foot forward that was crushed during an episode with one vile woman and a shovel. The woman still stood there, smoking and smiling as if her next customer would be coming soon. If only she knew that the next visitor would be me.

The woman just happened to turn around to look at the street behind me. She screamed. I grabbed the first thing in my reach, her hair. In her panic she put her cigarette in my arm. What was left of the flesh started to burn. She screamed louder as she watched the bubbles start to form in my skin. I felt no pain. It only made me want her more smelling her fear.

I started with her neck. It tasted sweeter than the last woman I had. The flesh came off in chunks. I swallowed some whole, while others I chewed. One of my bites hit her jugular vein, blood spurting everywhere. I showered my rotting tongue with her blood's juices. The redness made me think back to the strawberries I used to love when I was human.

She died almost immediately. I was thrilled about this as it gave me time to devour all the flesh I could of her. That's when I heard the noises, the loud noises, they were back. I dropped the woman, pieces of her flesh still hanging from my mouth. The shouting and vehicles again, humans were here.

I looked to my right and left. My one eye trying to focus as best as it could at the streets. The military had brought with them more civilians. They drove in any vehicle they could find. I was actually starting to panic, one thing I've never done when I was human.

I started dragging my legs to the nearest tree and hoped that they wouldn't see me. The woman's body would be evidence my kind was nearby. The men would check around her. This could be my last day, the day I'm finally caught. Could it be after all these years my final demise is a simple bullet from someone firing a gun for the first time?

The vehicles stopped. A few men got out of them and stepped forward. They looked around holding their guns up. I started to get worried. I hated this feeling. The men approached the woman's body.

"Yup, looks like one of them things already took out Besty," One of the men said.

I saw the others have a disgusted look on their faces. There were a few men in the vehicles yet, but I couldn't make out their faces. I stood still behind the tree and kept listening to the men discussing what they would be doing. I made sure not to turn around in case they would see me. If they did, my legs may not move fast enough to beat a bullet.

The men started to look around, but it was not where I stood, but further across the road. I started to get hopeful. I slowly turned my head to get a view of what the men were doing. Each one held their gun high and shouted at one another if they found one of my kind. Shots began to ring through the air and I saw some of my kind fall to the ground, swishing about with their last few minutes left.

I began to have another feeling I didn't have when I was human, sadness. The others like me just killed and shoved aside like waste. They weren't even as bad as those wretched women I so often killed. Some of them could even have been proper citizens at one time. It started to disgust me.

The men started to laugh as more shots were fired. It now seemed like a game to them to kill as many of my kind as they could. I wanted to go out there and stop them, chew on their flesh and spit them out. I knew I couldn't. The first sign of me and they would shoot. I'd be gone in a matter of four minutes, if that long. So I waited.

Some of the men went into the house I was at, slamming open the door and shooting without looking first. They must have found the man I chewed on earlier because I heard more yelling and more men running to the house. It was becoming clear that my time would be up soon.

I looked over at the woman now left alone. Her skin stained with her blood. Her neck opened by my jaws. The blood had stopped gushing out and a huge puddle was on the side of her body. She had tasted good. I felt good knowing my last meal was of something such as her, ridding the Earth of her was my greatest accomplishment.

It wouldn't be long now before they'd find me. I could only wait. After so many years of being this creature, so many years killing as a human, I was not surprised now that it would end like this. It almost seemed like some kind of justice. As if the victims of my human days were finally getting what they wanted. If that was true, then they must be laughing even in their deaths.

The men took a look at a car abandoned by the house. One I apparently didn't see. They started ripping apart the door and trashing the inside to see if they could find anything. I heard some sighs of annoyance. They didn't find anything. That was disappointing to me because I knew then their attention would be focused on my kind again.

They moved away from the car and I started to worry again. If I could still sweat I'd be certain pools of it would be falling off my forehead. I gathered up all I could. If I didn't move I'd be gone. If I did move I'd be gone. My idea was that I was going to get as many of those humans I could before they shot me.

I paced myself. It was going to be me against at least thirty and I knew that would be my ending. It was all I could do but stand there to get my courage up. Finally, to what seemed like hours but really only a few seconds, I made a run as fast as I could across the street. The men must have heard me and the shouting started.

I dragged my legs as quickly as I could to get to the people in the car. I heard some screaming and the gun shots started. In the one car were seated two men and a woman. The woman screamed some more. I went to her first. I did manage to get a taste of her arm before I felt the rupture in my head and fell down.

I had some time left and during that time I faintly heard the conversation two men were having.

"No, I'm sorry detective, it's 1919 there is no way that's him," the one man said.

"I'm sorry. I knew who it was back then. I just couldn't catch him. Seems like justice that I could this way," the other man replied.

"And because of the way this world is detective, no one will ever know that we just shot Jack the Ripper."

Independence Day:

The City

A loud cracking noise echoed through the field, another finger snapped off. Jim stared at Bob.

"I don't think you should be taking off any more fingers." Jim watched the undead thing grunt, trying to free itself from the leather straps that bound it to the tractor, trying to take a chunk out of Bob's flesh if it could just reach him.

"It's dead, what difference does it make?" Bob titled his head to the side avoiding the zombie's mouth opening and closing.

"Just doesn't seem right."

Bob grinned, taking his pliers, grabbed another one of the zombie's fingers and snapped it into two pieces, one of them falling to the ground. Jim watched as the finger disappeared between the wet blades of grass. The zombie grunted, its eyes coming alive filling with hatred.

#

Jim shook his head as he walked into the house.

"How did the day go?" Marsha asked.

Jim looked through the window at the darkened sky. He had been out with Bob for hours; nothing else besides harassing a zombie was accomplished for the day. Marsha looked at her exhausted husband. She sat down on one of the wooden chairs next to the table. She grabbed Jim's hand.

"How's about I make your favorite for dinner?"

Jim nodded. Marsha let go of her husband's hand as he sat down on the chair next to hers. She got up walked over to the stove.

"I don't think I can work on Bob's farm anymore." Jim wiped the sweat off his forehead. Marsha turned around.

"I thought you liked working with Bob."

"I used to, but what he is doing with these zombies is starting to bug me." Jim looked down at the dirt that covered his dry hands.

"But they're dead, what does it matter?" Marsha turned back to the counter where she started cutting some onions.

"I don't know. I mean I thought I saw something in its eyes."

"Like?" She continued cutting the onions.

"I don't know, maybe I'm going crazy, but I thought I saw anger."

"Anger, it can't feel honey, its dead."

"How do we know it can't feel? We have only recently known they existed."

"We know that they came from the surrounding city dear, the mistakes of the city are not ours to bear." She placed the onions in a bowl and turned on the stove. The light underneath the burner glowed.

Jim pounded his fist on the table. "It does not mean we have to treat them like slaves!" He stood up and walked over to the window that was in the corner from Marsha and looked out at the Bob's fields.

"If they don't feel anything and they're dead, what difference does it make?"

Jim sighed. "It's not right."

Marsha placed the onions in the pan, turned down the heat and turned around and walked by Jim. She placed a hand on his shoulder.

"We both know the city did something to those people. We also know they're dead. Doctor Grains confirmed it with one of the first that came here. You need to let this go Jim."

Jim turned. His eyes were dulled by the day's events.

"I can't. There is something about this that is all wrong. I can just feel it."

"Well, dinner will be done soon and then you can relax, okay?" Marsha took her hand off her husband's shoulder and went back to the stove. Jim just stood staring out the window.

#

"Get it out of here, burn it." Bob bent down and grabbed the dirty towel from the ground and wiped off his hands.

"Yes boss," Sam one of Bob's hired hands answered. He removed the torn zombie pieces and placed them into a plastic bag. He headed over to the makeshift bonfire pit that was set up for purposes of burning the zombies that Bob was done playing with; took some lit matches and dropped them into the pit. The pit caught fire immediately. In no time the flames were high. He dropped the bag into the pit and stood back and watched. The smell made his nose twitch.

Bob came up behind him.

"Well, how did it go?"

"No problems, boss." Sam continued to watch the flames burn and watch the small black cloud form.

"Why does that black cloud always come when you're burning these things?" Bob walked over to the edge of the bit and tried to look in without getting burnt.

Out of the pit came a burnt hand that grabbed Bob's arm. He screamed as he got pulled into the flames. Sam stood back in shock, barely keeping his footing. He turned quickly and ran back to the farm house, slammed open the door, and ran to get the rifle that Bob store in the closet. Sam watched the front door, expecting the thing from the pit to come out and go after him. His hands shook as he held the rifle pointed at the front entrance. A sudden noise startled him and he almost dropped the rifle.

"Who's there?" No one answered him. He

Sam moved back further as he sounds increased in volume. A mouth came at his neck and bit hard, blood spurted everywhere. Sam shoot the rifle as he fell down, a hole formed above and bits of ceiling fell to the floor. The zombie continued to munch on Sam, others soon followed behind the creature, each taking a portion of Sam for their own. They stopped for a moment to look at the arrival of some thing coming through the front door. The zombie was burnt, flesh barely on anything that was a skeleton. He grunted and the others stopped chewing on Sam and followed his lead out the door.

#

Jim walked over to the table and set his coffee down. He had decided he wasn't going over to Bob's farm to work today. It was early afternoon and he figured Bob would have called by now to ask where he was, but no calls. Jim shrugged his shoulders and sat down. Taking a sip of coffee, he looked out the window. He spit out his coffee and stood back up.

"What the hell?" He whispered to himself.

The sheriff and a few deputies' cars surrounded Bob's farmhouse.

"Marsha come here, you need to see this."

Marsha came out of the bathroom, combing out her still wet hair.

"Come here."

"What?" Marsha moved closer to Jim and looked out the window.

"What's going on?" Marsha squinted to see Bob's farmhouse.

"I don't know, you think we should go over there?"

Marsha continued to focus on the police cars and people entering and leaving the house.

"Maybe." She continued to brush her hair.

"Fine, I'll go and let you know what happened." Jim turned and walked out of the house.

The sirens were deafening. Jim walked slowly across the driveway and got into his truck. It started with a few hisses and then he was off. A few minutes later he was in front of Bob's farmhouse.   He climbed out of his truck, one of the deputies came up to him.

"Hey Jim," the deputy said.

"Hey, Boris, what's going on here?"

Boris looked at him oddly. "You don't know?"

Jim shook his head.

"Okay, well, Sam is dead."

"Sam? How?" Jim looked at the front door where he saw some men putting a white sheet over something, blood staining the cotton fabric.

"Your guess is as good as mine. One of Bob's workers found him about an hour ago and called it in. Jim it is beyond anything I've seen in these parts."

"What do you mean?"

"He was ripped into pieces." Boris looked down.

"He was what?" Jim's eyes widened.

"Ripped into several parts."

"I heard what you said, but what could do such a thing?" As soon as Jim said it he knew.

"Did you know Bob kept a large cage in the back of his house?"

"No, I didn't."

"Well, we found it while searching. It's huge. It looks like he was keeping some animals in there."

"Not sure if they were the type of animals you're thinking of Boris."

Boris dropped the cigarette that burned to the filter while talking to Jim and stepped on the butt, stomping into the grass.

"What are you talking about?"

"Them things that came here from the city."

"They're harmless, stupid too."

"No, Bob used to tease them, torture if you will."

Boris looked at the farmhouse and back at Jim.

"They're dead, what difference does it make?"

Jim sighed. "Do you know how many times I've heard that? It doesn't matter? I saw him torturing one day. I saw the look in the creature's eyes. It was angry. It was as if it could feel and know what Bob was doing."

"Jim, I know Sam here getting killed is a shock, but you're going way over your head with ideas like these."

"Boris!" Jim slammed his fist on the hood of his truck.

"Jim, calm down. I'll take it into consideration, but both you and I know none of the boys over there, including the sheriff will believe you, now if you have any information, give me a call." Boris left and went back inside the farmhouse.

Jim stood there for a moment rubbing the back of his hand. He shook his head. He just knew it was the zombies and knowing Bob, those cages were for holding them. Jim got back into his truck and drove home. As he pulled into the gravel driveway his attention was drawn to the busted front door. He quickly got of the truck and ran inside. He was greeted by a sharp cooking knife. He held up his hands.

"Marsh, it's me, put the knife down."

Marsh took a second look at her husband and let go of the knife.

"Jim, it was awful. They killed the dog."

"Who honey?" Jim wrapped his arms around her and pulled her into his chest.

"Them dead things, they came here. They got through the door. I happened to see them as I was coming out of the bedroom. Jim I didn't hear them. I was using the hairdryer." She sobbed loudly.

"Honey, it's not your fault, ssh." He rubbed her hair with his hand. She pulled away from him.

"What are we going to do?" She wiped her eyes and looked at Jim.

Jim stood frozen.

"Jim?"

He shook himself out of his daze and looked down at Marsh.

"We are getting out of here."

"To where?"

"The city."

"Do you think they'll be back?"

"I don't know. However, they came from the city so there has to be some answers on how we get rid of them."

Marsha started to move back.

"But won't we be going into the heart of it?"

"Perhaps, but I'm hoping there are still some parts that aren't infected."

"I don't know."

Jim moved closer to Marsha and grabbed her hand.

"You have to trust me."

"That's what you said when you wanted to move here."

He smiled.

"When do we leave?" She let go of Jim's hand.

"Now."

They both ran to the truck and got inside.

Another hissing sound signaled the truck was ready to go and Jim stomped on the accelerator pedal, dust and stones flew up from the gravel driveway.

#

By nighttime, Jim and Marsha were in the start of the city of Farnhooth. The city was renamed after news reporters started gathering the story of the first outbreak of dead people or zombies, it ended up sticking. They pulled into an abandoned gas station.

"I'm still not sure about this." Marsha looked at the building that had its front door busted, glass pieces still on the ground along with shredded papers everywhere.

Jim got out of the truck.

"Where are you going?"

"Going to find some guns."

"At a gas station?"

"When the outbreak first happened, don't you remember reading that they were selling guns everywhere to help people.'

"No, I don't remember."

"Okay, well, I need to get some. Now that we know they are dangerous and not what was originally thought by us, I need something to protect us."

"But shooting them, are you sure that will work." She placed her hands on the door and turned her head out the window.

"I saw Bob do it once. He shot one clear in the head. It went down and never came up."

"Are you sure?"

"Marsha listen, this is our only hope if we are going to go further into the city. Now we also know why we never got any more news from them." He looked down and shuffled his feet, dreading getting the guns.

"Okay, but hurry."

Jim nodded and ran into the gas station. Glass shards were over the counter along with papers scattered everywhere. He pushed some of the papers aside to see into the counter. A part of it was already busted and he looked into it. There were a few 9 mms and a couple of shotguns. He pulled them out placing two 9 mms into his pockets and the shotguns under one of his arms. Jim moved some other little trinkets out of the way and came across some ammo. He grabbed what he needed, balancing them in his hands, and moved quickly out of the gas station. Marsha got out of the truck and opened his door. Jim placed the ammo and guns in their small back seat. He took a couple of rounds out and placed them into the two 9 mms he pulled back out of his pockets, making sure they were ready he climbed back into the truck.

The city almost looked like a ghost town; buildings were empty and only a few people walked around. Jim parked the truck along side the curb in front of the old tool store. He got out of the truck taking with him the two guns. He placed one in the back of his pants and carried the other.

"Where are we going?" Marsha asked.

"Somewhere on this street if I remember from when we did get news from the city, there is a clinic. The clinic is where the first cases were diagnosed."

"And?"

"And perhaps we can find out through the records what brought the infection on and perhaps somewhere in all that medical garbage we can find the answers we need."

Jim walked further down the sidewalk carrying the gun in one hand and Marsha's hand in his other. They walked into a white building that had only a few letters remaining on the front marking it as a clinic. Jim let go of Marsha's hand and pointed the gun in front of him, turning in every direction to see what if anything was around.

"There's some folders over there." Marsha pointed in front of them.

"Okay, you stay close behind, I'll lead."

Jim walked closer to the folders on the wall; some had fallen to the floor in what looked like wind storm had it the area.

"You start grabbing any files and page through them." Jim turned around and faced the opposite direction of Marsha pointing the gun in front of him. Marsha grabbed a few files and placed them on the desk on her right. One folder stood out to her. It was marked 'Project Dead.'

"Jim, come here I think I have something."

Jim moved back and turned around leaning in to take a quick look.

"What is Project Dead?"

Marsha opened the folder and flipped through some of the papers had charts, some prescription forms and information on the diagnosis. She handed the two sheets to Jim.

"Do you know how to use one of these?" He held up the gun to Marsha.

"Now is a better time than any." She grabbed the gun from Jim and pointed the gun out toward the entrance.

Jim started to read the first document labeled 'Beginning.'

"It says here that this was an experimental project that started with cows."

"Cows?" Marsha asked not turning around.

"Yeah, cloning of cows."

"I thought cloning was banned?"

"Apparently, this clinic thought they had something that would impress the Federal Government to think otherwise."

"Interesting."

"Thought you would like that. It also says here that most of the patients didn't make it through the first trial with the injection."

"What injection?" Marsha kept the gun steady, focused on the opened door.

"An injection of some drug here, can't pronounce it, but it was one that helped to reproduce the DNA in cows. They tried the drug on humans. The humans died from it. Then there is a strange thing down here that they have marked with a question mark."

"What?"

"Some notes about certain people dying and then breaking out of their graves and moving around."

"Did they think it has to do with the injections?"

"It doesn't say, but putting two and two together and I'm not too bad at math, I would assume they were wondering."

A crashing noise brought both their attention to the front door. In came four zombies, some had fresh blood dripping from their mouths. Marsha fired a couple of times. She hit one in the head and it went down; the second she missed completely.

"Let's go!" Jim yelled grabbing her arm and running with the folder in one hand.

Marsha shot as they went. She wasn't so bad at shooting, if only she would hit her mark more often. They found a door leading to an adjoining building. Jim kicked it open and they both ran into a room.

"Now what?" Marsha said turning around to face the open door and waiting for the zombies to come through.

Jim looked around. The building was structured in a strange zigzag pattern. He saw a door leading to the outside of that building.

"Over here, door, go."

They both ran as fast as they good to the glass door. Jim pushed it open with his right shoulder, Marsha followed. Jim turned and shut the door. He found an old table by the side of the building. He put the folder on the ground and shoved the table slowly against the door.

"I hope this works."

Marsha nodded. They ran around the other side of the building and looked around the corner to make sure none of the zombies were by their truck. After seeing the coast was clear, they made their way down the sidewalk and climbed into the truck. Jim started the truck and they squealed their way down the road. As they went past the front of the clinic they could see the zombies slowly walking or stumbling was more like it, out of the clinic's front entrance onto the street.

"Here read this." Jim handed Marsha the folder and she put the gun in the middle of the seat.

"It says here that they may have found another drug to combat this 'weird disease' as they called it here.

"But they weren't sure it was caused by them?"

"Reading further down, they now seemed pretty certain. They had apparently run some tests on a few patients who had been killed after becoming part of the walking dead population."

"And?"

"And well it seems here that the cow DNA and the human DNA made some weird chemical in their bodies, which their immune system could not handle. Once they died, most people got buried. Then one night according to what they say in their files, they came back."

"But what about a treatment, does it say anything about that?"

Marsha moved her finger down the document as she read.

"Um, wait, here maybe something. That sounds disgusting though."

"What?"

"It says something here that feeding them dead things human manure seemed to stop the disease and then they could truly die for good."

"You mean human crap is the cure?" Jim's brow creased. He pushed his hair back with one hand.

"Um, yeah, according to the test results and judging from the charts, and I'm no medical chart reader, but pretty simply said, it did."

Jim rubbed his chin and turned the wheel to the right, leading them back to their town.

"Great, so in order to keep those things from eating us, we need to feed them crap. And where are we going to get a bunch of human crap from?"

"Maybe the sewer plant?" Marsha rolled her eyes at her husband.

"Ah, maybe we can go to the sewer plant."

"What a great idea." Marsha smiled to herself.

They drove until they reached the border of the town. There stood the sewer plant.

"I do have a question. How are we going to get this manure where them creatures are?"

Jim looked around.

"All I can think of is that somehow we release what's stored in there."

"Throughout the whole town? You know what kind of smell that would produce?"

"I'd rather smell that for years than worry about being dead or even coming back from the dead."

"Fine, what do I call you, manure leader?" Marsha said as they got out of the truck.

"I was thinking along the lines of Obi-One Crap Master."

They both laughed and walked to the door of the sewer plant. It was left open by one of the employees which was nice for them since it had a code lock.

Jim walked over to the back room. A control panel with several colored buttons was positioned near the wall.

"Will that help?"

"I can't see in harm in trying." Jim started pushing any button that said release or pump. A loud cranking noise was heard after each button.

A strong odor started coming into the room.

"Bingo, I think we hit something." Jim pushed another button, same noise and same smell.

Marsha ran to the door and looked outside. It was like a huge fudge sundae, however it wasn't fudge.

"It's working," she screamed over the noise.

A banging noise was heard that was slight, but still grabbing her attention.

"Jim!"

Jim turned quickly and saw a dozen zombies coming toward the front door. Their movement was slow, but they had smelled live flesh.

"The crap, or manure should be getting to them." Jim hurriedly pushed some more buttons.

"Jim they're getting closer."

Jim looked once more at the opening seeing the dead things creep up to where they were standing. One managed to get in through the door and Marsha ran to Jim.

"Quick, shoot it!"

"I can't. I forgot the gun."

Jim looked at her with shock.

"You didn't bring it?"

"In all the chaos, no I forgot." She sighed heavily.

#

The human manure continued to poor outside onto the grass and filtering into the road. Thunder was heard outside and soon large drops of rain carried the manure further into other areas of town. Zombies that were in the stream of the manure fell instantly, dissolving like indigestion tablets in water. The town was rid of any walking dead and the city that had few people in the same, just a strong odor was present for several years afterwards and most houses were sold within a few days after the sewage plant somehow spilled a bunch of manure.

Marsha and Jim, what happened to them was beyond a miracle. The manure had splattered into the room they were in. The zombies that managed to get in by them were caught in the manure and died instantly. Jim and Marsha had to walk through the manure to get to his truck, driving was difficult through the thick muck, but they managed. They went as far as three cities away before they escaped the manure. When they went to the hotel to stay the night until they figured out their next move, the owner had addressed a strange smell to one of his employees.

Skin Care

The girl's forearm skin flapped against the back of the wooden chair. Charles smiled as he looked at his precise cutting skills. He put the bloody knife down on the table next to the chair. His nails were filled with skin fragments of the girl. He placed them in the wash bowl that sat on the table. Charles watched as the blood off his hands floated in the water.

"Charles, did you want me to serve the white wine we picked up earlier this month from Mrs. James?" His wife Sara said.

"That would be delightful darling. I'm almost done here and then we can have our fried steaks." He smiled as she walked out of the room back into the kitchen.

Charles took the piece of freshly cut arm flesh, took his long knife, poked a hole in it and dipped it in the water. It was important that the flesh stay as clean as possible. He dipped it in and out until all the loose blood was gone. Grabbing the flesh, he placed it on the cloth on the table. Charles moved the cloth over the flesh and pulled from it any dirt that got trapped on either side.

The girl is sitting on the wooden chair. Her eyes have a vacant stare. Her shirt tore at the location where Charles cut it. The rest of her body limps from the shock and loss of blood. Charles turns to look over at her. He knows that the flesh will only stay fresh for a short time. The arm flesh falls back down on the cloth and Charles walks over to the girl.

"Now we have to take care of the meat properly," Charles said to the dead girl. He picked up the body and dragged it into the walk-in freezer located in the back of the room.

The girl's body fell limp against the freezer wall. Only twenty-one, the girl had come to visit Charles and his wife for a night away at their bed and breakfast. Charles took the hose that was hooked up on the side, turned the water on and started to spray her down making sure any dirt or particles were off her half-naked body. It helped to also freeze her body quicker. When he was satisfied, he turned off the hose and closed the freezer door behind him.

Charles walked back to the table and grabbed the arm flesh with the cloth it laid in. He walked to the kitchen where Sara was.

"I got some good meat this time." He smiled at her.

"I'm sure our guests will enjoy their meals tonight." She grinned and took the flesh from Charles. Placing it on the counter, she took a knife and cut it into small sections. The hot frying pan provided the perfect bed for the sections to cook in. Sara added a bit of salt, pepper and some extra garlic cloves into the mix. She breathed in the aroma.

"Oh Charles, the food smells so good." Sara moved the flesh around in the frying pan, turning it over every so often.

"We got some good stuff this time; young and tender." Charles grinned.

"Yes, we lucked out." Sara put down the spatula, turned to the cupboards and took out six blue plates for their guests.

Charles uncorked the white wine, placed it on the counter and got some glasses to pour it in. He poured the wine, filling the glasses part way. Setting the wine bottle down, he turned to look at the vegetables steaming in the pot on the other burner. Sara walked over to the pot and grabbed the sides with two hot-pads. She strained the vegetables and placed them in a large bowl.

"I believe we're done," Sara said cheerfully. Charles nodded.

They took the plates out to the guests sitting at the table in the dinning area. Sara took a plate, one at a time and placed it in front of the guests.

"Something smells good coming from the kitchen," one of the woman said to Sara. Sara smiled at her.

"We hope you like it. It's our house fried steak, guests have raved about it."

Everyone smiled. Charles brought out the fried steak on the plate to serve. He took his serving fork and began placing a piece on everyone's plate.

"This looks so delicious," a man said who was sitting at the end of the table.

"Trust me, it's to die for," Charles said as he watched Sara go to the kitchen and come back with the steamed vegetables. She quickly served them to the guests.

Charles went back to the kitchen and came back with the wine. He sat down the glasses, one in front of each guest. He smiled at everyone and sat down at the other end of the table. Sara moved a chair close to him and sat down as well.

"Hmm, this is great. I must commend you two for such an extraordinary meal," the one woman who wore a red hat and a red skirt said.

"Why thank you," Sara said taking a bite of the fried steak she sliced up. Charles smiled at her and took his own bite of the steak.

"We were lucky to come across such fine meat," Charles replied after taking some of the steamed vegetables and placing them into his mouth.

The guests finished their meal, thanked the two and proceeded to go upstairs to their room.

"That went well," Charles said after the guests were gone. He patted his mouth gently with a napkin.

"How much meat do we have off of this one?" Sara asked Charles as she stood up and gathered the plates together.

"I say some good breast meat, perhaps another couple of meals with fried steaks off the arm and some thigh meat." He stood up and gathered some of the glasses.

"Not a lot then?"

"No, wasn't that much on this one."

"Well, that means we have to get some more meat. Who's on the date book for upcoming stays?" She asked as she took the plates to the kitchen. Charles followed carrying the glasses.

"I don't know but I can find out." He placed the

glasses on the counter and went to the front entrance where the date book was kept.

Charles paged through the dates of the upcoming visits. He noticed a woman and man staying the next night at the bed and breakfast. They were both staying separately and alone.

"Perfect," he whispered to himself. He made a mental note on the two names and went to tell Sara.

Sara was busying putting plates and silverware into the dishwasher.

"Honey, I believe we found our next supply of meat." Charles had a smile that went from ear to ear. Sara turned around.

"Oh?"

"Yes, two travelers coming in alone tomorrow. It is extreme luck."

They looked at each other and laughed.

#

It was early the next day. Some of the guests from the previous night were leaving. Charles said his goodbyes to them and they once again complemented him on his meal the night before. The new guests arrived slowly for the night's stay. Each one Charles greeted and showed them their rooms. The two guests who were staying alone came later than he had hoped, but did come. First was the woman.

He smiled as she approached the desk.

"Hi, my name is Sally Higgers. I have a reservation for tonight." She peered over at the date book, scanning to see her name there.

"Yes, right here." Charles smiled at her.

"Great. When is dinner normally served?"

"Around eight," Charles replied.

"Oh good, gives me a chance to do some reading."

Charles grinned as he knew that reading was the last thing she would be doing. She took the key from him and went upstairs with her bag that she had insisted that she carry by herself.

Charles went back by Sara who was putting books on the shelves for the guests in case they wanted to read.

"Sally Higgers is here."

"Who is that?" Sara asked.

"One of our alone visitors." Charles grinned.

"Oh!" Sara yelled excitedly.

"Yes I know. I'm going to wait until the other guests get a bit settled, shouldn't be too long now."

Sara nodded and put the last book on the shelf. Charles sat down in one of the chairs they put out for guests in the reading room. He waited until everything settled down. There were only a few guests who had arrived making the trip up the stairs easier for Charles. He avoided any opened doors where the guests sat waiting, putting away clothes or staring out at the beautiful garden just outside their windows.

Sally Higgers was putting away her clothes. Her back was facing the entrance to the room. Charles stood by the entrance breathing quietly like a hunter waiting for his prey. He waited, watched as Sally's arms shown through the sleeves of her dress. Sally continued to put clothes in the dresser; allowing Charles to see the full frame of her body. She would make at least a few meals given her weight. He smiled. Slowly he approached her from behind; the knife in his hand that pointed at her neck. Most of the time he enjoyed playing with his food, watching as they squirmed and screamed "no"; tonight though, they had a full house and he didn't have time.

Sally turned just in time to feel the knife dig in slowly across her throat. She didn't have time to scream, but her widened eyes showed the fear. Grabbing her neck for the final time, she fell to the floor. The blood gurgled out of her neck quickly. A small puddle formed underneath her neck. The carpet was stained now. Charles knew the carpet would need to be replaced, as they often did when these types of killings were needed.

Charles turned around and shut the door quietly. There was no need to disturb the other guests. Getting Sally down would be a challenge, but not one in which Charles could not handle. In the closet was a set of bags, bags that could carry a body. Guests would ask what the bags were for, Charles and Sara simply told them it had to do with storage. Like his mother had always told him 'it was better to be prepared for anything.'

The closet opened with ease and Charles grabbed the cloth bag. He pushed the opening of the bag under her feet and pulled at the bag while lifting the body up just a tad to make sure it was a secure fit. He smiled. Sara would love to make some pot roast with some of this meet. The guests would enjoy another wonderfully cooked dinner. After the body was secured in the bag, he zipped its sides up. Looking around, Charles made sure that he took the bag, placed it over his shoulder and locked the door on his way out making sure no one would go in the room.

Charles watched as he walked down the stairs, careful steps assured him that he wouldn't drop the body by mistake. Some of the guests passed him by in the front room as he walked by with the large bag. They smiled at him and kept talking to each other. Charles grinned. He often wondered just how much people paid attention to their surroundings. The body hit his back up and down as he continued to walk back to the butchering room. A push of a button and the door opened and he walked through.

The other woman whom they had such a great meal
the night before, still was frozen in the walk-in freezer,
that meet he had chosen for a later date, but not too late
or the meat would not remain fresh. Charles took the bag
and put it across his wooden cutting table. On the walls
behind the table stood his butchering tools, a knife, a saw,
tongs, a sword, apron and several other items that
dangled on hooks for his visual pleasure.

He unzipped the bag and looked at the woman. The
cut had gashed a long bloody line against her neck. The
cut was thought of just so as to not damage any meat.
Charles removed the bag from underneath her, took
some water and started to wash the neck wound and any
droplets of blood that had dripped down with a cloth. He
took a scissors and starting to cut her shirt at the sleeve
and across her breasts. The shirt fell off and dangled on
the table. The rest of her clothes came off with ease. A
few snips here and there.

He dumped the cloth back into the water bowl and
washed the rest of the naked woman's body. After he
was satisfied she was clean enough, he reached over her
and took a knife off the hook. The butcher knife he held

in his hand, was his precise cutting tool. The tool he slightly cut the skin with, making sure not to get any organs below it. It was if he was a fisherman and he was filleting his fish; however, he liked to think of himself more as a butcher, taking prime sections of the meat.

The first cut produced a small amount of blood as he punctured her skin. He pulled the knife across her leg taking off about two inch wide piece of flesh off her thigh. The pieces of thigh were put on top of another cloth he had on the right side of the woman's body. Soon the sections were stacking up. He looked at the woman knowing there were several choice pieces of meat left to cut.

He took these pieces of thigh and washed them in the sink across from the table. Drying them off ever so gently, Charles put them into a plastic container for storage. He went back to the woman's body and looked at her fingers. Taking one finger at a time while holding up her right hand, he noticed how large her bones were. The bones would make for good soup mixings. He cracked the index finger as if he was cracking crab to eat. Charles grabbed another plastic square container and put the bone pieces in there. He had made sure the skin was removed carefully first.

After a few minutes all the finger skin and finger bones were removed. They were placed along with the rest in the container. He smiled at his good fortune with this one. Charles went back to the woman and looked at her. A few more slices here and there for breast meet, drum sticks and some more arm slices, would set up meals for about a week. He continued cutting the legs with precise skill; each time cleaning his knife off with the wet cloth. The meat was as clean as it could be and placed into more containers. Sara would be so thrilled.

The sections of leg meat he could not place in the containers, he took over to the grinder and ground it up. Hamburgers were also a specialty of Sara's and he knew she couldn't wait to make more of them. When the leg sections were ground into fine meat, he shut the grinder off. The grinder shrilled its motor off. He looked into the bowl. The meat was just perfect. He estimated about a pounds worth. The bowl was pulled from underneath the grinder. Charles placed it on the table next to the other containers.

He grabbed one of the plastic bags and placed the bowl in it. In another bag, the rest of the containers and set them aside. Charles studied the girl's body that was skinned in any area he could find. Looking her up and down, he noticed he had completely stripped her of any meat left on her bones. He grinned at this. All his containers were filled with choice, grade A meat.

Charles took the woman's body and placed it on the conveyer belt they had they went into the fire bin. It would only take a few minutes before the woman's remains would turn to ash. He watched making sure that none of her body remained unburned. After the last of the ashes dropped into the bin on the other side, Charles turned off the belt and went to grab the bags.

He walked out the door, pressed a few buttons on the lock pad and walked to the kitchen. Sara stood over the stove cooking vegetables.

"So what were you able to get this time?" She turned and asked Charles.

"You'll love this darling. I have some ground meat for hamburgers." He smiled as he handed her the bag with the bowl of ground flesh in it. She smiled.

"Wonderful, how's about we have that tonight?" She placed the bowl on the counter and stirred the oil in the frying pan.

"That would be delightful. I'm sure our guests will love your famous burgers." Charles placed the other containers in the refrigerator.

"Will you please take out the plates? They're already sitting out there."

Charles nodded and opened the cupboard to get the red, stripped patterned plates. He took them and walked out to the dinning room. The guests were chatting about anything and everything including the expected dinner.

"What's on the menu?" the man asked that sat on the right side. His shoes dirty from his nightly run.

"Hamburgers." Charles smiled and placed the plates in front of them.

"Ah, that's what that wonderful smell is coming from the kitchen," the man replied.

Sara came out sometime later with a serving plate full of burgers and buns. Everyone made a mock cheering noise. She placed a burger a piece on the guests' plates.

No sooner than she had set them down, the guests were diving into them. She smiled at them and at her husband. He had done such a good job with the meat this time, as he always did.

She started to remember when they first started producing their own meat. It was such a thrill to know that people enjoyed the taste and that the cost was so much cheaper than going to the bulk markets. The bed and breakfast she inherited from her Aunt was the perfect place to practice this new money saving skill. It worked well. Sara cooked and Charles did the butcher work.

#

"Are you sure you weren't imagining things sir?" The policeman asked the man sitting across from him.

"No, I'm sure. I saw them. I saw them take what looked like pieces of human flesh and cook them."

"Sir, we know Sara and Charles. They have been members of this community for years. They wouldn't hurt a fly." The policeman took a puff off his cigarette. The man glared at him.

"So you're telling me you're not going to do anything?" The man asked angrily as he leaned over the officer's desk.

"I think what you need to do is get some rest. The accident you had was pretty severe. Those roads from the bed and breakfast are horrendous."

The man slammed his right fist on the table, got up and stormed out of the police station. The officer just shook his head.

#

A man walked into the bed and breakfast. He was booked for a single room for the night. Another man waited behind a desk to greet him.

"Welcome to our bed and breakfast. We hope you enjoy your stay. We serve breakfast and a wonderful dinner; both made by my very talented wife."

"That sounds amazing," the man replied.

"It certainly is." Charles smiled and handed the man his room key.

They Crawled

They crawled, they flew and they stung. All the things Mary hated about bugs.

"I don't want to go," Mary whined. Roy rolled his eyes.

"Sweetie, now listen, it's just a camping trip. We'll be in tents." He walked over to her and placed his hand on her shoulder.

"I hate bugs." She frowned and looked down at the floor where her left foot made a circle on the carpet.

"It'll be fine. I even have bug spray." Roy held up a can of bug spray. Mary looked up, nodded briefly and went back to starting at her foot.

"How long is this trip again?" Mary looked up at Roy who had turned to put the spray in the bag.

"Just a couple of days. Neil and Joanne will be there later."

"Fine, whatever. I'm going to take a shower before we leave." She walked into the bathroom and shut the door hard.

Roy continued packing.

"All set to leave honey, don't be too long," he yelled. All that was heard in response was a loud grunt.

***

The side roads were a bit rough getting to the camping park. Mary sighed.

"It'll be just a few more minutes and then we'll be there," Roy said with a grin.

"Yippee." Mary turned to look out the passenger's window.

"Look, we're here." Roy turned the car into the narrow road that went into the camping area.

"What kind of name is *Feel Good Camping*?" Mary asked sarcastically. Roy laughed.

"It's supposed to make you feel good. You know release the stress?" He gently nudged her shoulder.

"Yeah, sure, I'd rather be at work." Mary unsnapped her buckle and opened the door.

"You know your work stresses you out too much." Roy opened his door, stepped out and looked at the area.

"Well at least being a surgeon is a lot better than sitting here for two days getting bitten by bugs, not showering and listening to Neil whine about his work."

Roy turned back to look at her.

"It's not so bad."

"We'll see." Mary walked over to the spot they had reserved for their tent.

The grass was cut short, some of it brown from the heat and no watering. Mary pushed her shoe through the thin layer of dirt that was under the old picnic bench. Roy approached with their tent all bunched up in his arms.

"Want to help me?" He smiled at her. She nodded.

The tent went up quickly and they both sat down on the grass outside of it.

"Whew." Roy pretended to wipe sweat off his forehead. Mary laughed.

"It's good to see you laugh."

Mary smiled. They turned as they heard loud music and the beeping of a car horn.

"Hey!" The woman in the passenger side of the red Explorer yelled out to Mary and Roy.

Mary waved. Roy got up and waited for the Explorer to pull up besides his car. Neil shut the car off, opened the door and stepped out. Joanne followed.

"Hey man, how's it going?" Neil asked Roy. Roy grinned.

"Are we going to have fun here or what?" Roy laughed.

Mary sighed and got up. Joanne was already walking over by her.

"Hi, Joanne," Mary said. Her voice was low and raspy from the dryness outside.

"Hey Mary." Joanne smiled.

"I'm not sure if I'm ready for this." Mary looked down at the grass again. The tent swayed a bit in the small breeze.

"Come on Mary, it's not a big deal. It's just a hike through the woods up the way."

"I know, but I hate bugs." She turned to look at Roy and Neil laughing at something Neil said about his work again.

"Geez Mary, it's not like we are going to be dealing with any kind of mutated insects or anything." Joanne rolled her eyes. Mary grunted.

"You two ready?" Roy said and grabbed the bag out of the car.

"I guess." Mary turned to Joanne and she nodded. They walked over by the men.

Roy gestured for them to follow and they all started walking up the small dirt path leading to the woods. The trail was upwards and the trees started to line up on each side.

The woods were huge in the park, spreading across what seemed like miles. Mary scuffled across the path.

She didn't want to be there and had no problem letting everyone know that.

"We should be off this path soon and in the central part of the woods," Roy said turning to check on Mary every so often.

"These woods are beautiful. What kind of bird is that?" Joanne pointed to one of the bigger trees on the left.

"No idea, never see anything that big before." Neil's eyes squinted to see. He tried to move closer to where the bird was perched on the branch. The bird cawed. The sound echoed throughout the woods, shaking some of the trees nearby.

"What the…" Roy turned to look at the tree.

"Did you see it?" Joanne kept pointing to the tree.

"I didn't see anything," Mary replied sarcastically.

"I know you heard that." Neil stared at Mary.

"Shut-up, I said I heard nothing." Mary's voice started to rise.

"Okay, enough you two. Maybe it's just a bird from this country. None of us have seen every type of bird in this world. Have we?" Roy turned to look around at everyone. They all nodded in agreement.

"Fine," Neil muttered under his breath.

The four of them kept walking, ignoring the loud cawing from the bird they just saw. The trees were getting bigger the further down the path they went.

"I really don't like this." Joanne looked around the trees on either side of her. She started to sweat down her forehead.

"I agree for once." Mary followed closely behind.

"Come on you two, there's nothing to worry about." Roy continued on the path. It started leaning upwards.

"Roy, hey man, this is really freaking me out." Neil turned around to look at the darkness that crept in.

"I told you didn't I that there wasn't anything to worry about. Will you listen?" Roy laughed. Neil didn't laugh with him.

Joanne and Mary followed behind. Mary stopped to look at the tree that stood on her right. Its leaves were wilted and the branches were black.

"I'm no tree expert, and maybe it's the darkness, but are trees supposed to look like this." Mary pointed at the tree. She drew back her hand quickly. It was cold by the draft that swiftly went past.

"I would have to agree." Joanne stared at the same tree. Neil came back to look as well.

"Everything seems to be dying." Mary bent down on the ground and saw little squirrels on their backs, dead.

"Roy, what is this place?" Joanne asked. She rubbed her arm.

"It's the woods, just like I told you." Roy was almost up the whole path.

"Roy, I don't want to go any further," Joanne pleaded. Mary stared at her, then looked at Neil.

The three of them waited for Roy's response, which didn't come.

"Roy?" Mary asked up the path. There was no answer.

"Oh, man, now what?" Neil asked. He was shivering too.

The trees surrounding them started to sway; branches and leaves falling all around them.

"We need to get out of her," Joanne whispered.

"But we need to find Roy." Mary started up the path; legs worn from the walking and her hands almost numb from the cold.

Neil and Joanne followed. Mary looked further on but didn't see Roy anywhere. The trees were starting to disappear. A clearing was up ahead. The darkness was overwhelming.

"I can't see anything," Joanne whispered.

"Here take this." Neil handed her a flash light.

Joanne pointed the flash light directly into the clearing. She screamed.

"What is it?" Mary asked running to her side.

Joanne remained frozen. The flash light still pointed at the clearing.

"Oh my God." Neil walked closer to get a better view.

Surrounding them were stacks of bodies. They were all layered together. Joanne screamed again and Neil gagged. Mary remained where she was.

"What the …"

Roy suddenly appeared.

"Do you like what I've done here?" He grinned.

'What?" Mary turned to look at Roy, then back at the bodies.

"This is my play ground for Jokey." He gestured with his hands around the clearing.

"What's a Jokey?" Mary asked. Her skin got colder as she stood there.

"Jokey is my friend." Roy turned around and looked at a big termite walking over to the others.

"A bug, you did this?" Mary ran behind the others.

"For you honey, I wanted you to get rid of your fear of bugs."

"By this!" Mary turned to run down the path. The bug came after her.

"Mary, you're offending Jokey, come back!" Roy yelled after her. Neil and Joanne stood there.

"Roy, how?" Joanne asked.

"By simply giving it what it wanted." Roy grinned.

"What was that?" Neil asked looking around. His eyes widened as he saw the bodies again.

"By this…" Roy held up a bottle of Miracle Grow.

"What the…" Neil said shocked.

"Now who says regular gardening tools can't help with anything else?" Roy laughed.

Mary's screams could be heard through out the forest.

They Know

It started one day; the cold sweats, the waking up in the middle of the night. Ryan couldn't shake the headaches. The headaches that started once his father died and he inherited the family business, the funeral home. He dreaded going there when he was a teenager and now years later he was the owner.

He had watched his father put make-up on the dead people. It made Ryan feel disgusted. Yet even with all the work he watched his father do, a certain interest started to brew in the money aspect of the business. The people would come in to the funeral home request arraignments for their loved ones and pay the costs. Ryan soon discovered that funeral costs were high. When he took over the funeral home he made a choice to make money from death an easier way, killing them himself instead of waiting for the corpses to come to him.

The first killing was not as hard as Ryan had thought. It was really a simple situation. He waited as the young woman walked down the street. It was dark and she was alone. He came from behind her and slit her throat, took her bag and made it look like a robbery gone wrong. No one had suspected Ryan.

In the city where he slit the woman's throat, bad things always happened. Soon enough the body was looked over for any evidence and then sent to Ryan's funeral home. The family paid big bucks to have her made over and make the necessary arrangements for the huge funeral that would follow.

It was this first killing that Ryan felt his headaches go away. It was also where he had figured it was so simple that he would pursue future victims. The money was so much that he made a choice to hire an assistant. One that would have no clue how the money was made. It was really for professional purposes to show the community he did not work alone.

He found Lina one day at a bookstore. She was looking at books that dealt with death. Soon after he met her, they sat down at the café part of the store and talked.

He found out she always wanted to be a funeral director. Ryan found that odd for anyone to want, especially a woman. He invited her to work with him and she had been with him ever since.

They had worked well together. She learned everything from Ryan and when there were new techniques to be learned, she would be the first to go to the conventions. Lina was always excited to share the new information with Ryan who simply nodded and went back to prepping whatever dead person he was working on at the time.

She then would come in at night even with some strange friends she had met. Ryan always watched these friends of hers come in with their weird necklaces and books that they always wrote on when they were in the funeral home. Ryan eventually asked her not to bring them anymore. Lina reluctantly agreed and they never showed up again. It was after that time that Ryan started to notice Lina going off more on her own, doing things in private, but there was never a reason to mistrust her.

#

He walked the cold cement floor. Ryan sighed and opened the big steel door that entered into the room where he prepared the dead bodies. A job in itself he found disturbing.

Ryan moved his neck side to side and put on his plastic coat gear as to not get anything on his clothes. He hated the times when he first started all the garbage that would come at him spraying out of the dead bodies ruining his expensive suits. Ryan had learned quickly to use the plastic gear every other Funeral Director wore. In this particular case, he wore the plastic suit only as a formality as one of his assistants had already embalmed the woman one of the things Ryan hated the most.

The corpse was flat on the metal table in front of him. He took the make-up kit on the counter next to the table. Ryan smacked his lips and swallowed hard trying to keep the disgusting taste that came from his stomach as he looked on at the dead body. The woman was ugly and he thought even uglier upon death. Why did he have to do this? There was no way he could make this woman look any better.

He started with a foundation that gave the ash-colored woman some more life to her face. She stared at him with an intense focus that only the dead could have. Ryan took his right index finger and shut her eyelids. He couldn't take her staring at him as if it was his fault she was dead. She deserved everything she got and then some.

Her family, mostly just her mother and her sister would be in soon to view her and give Ryan the clothes he needed to dress her for the funeral. He hated the families, always crying and wanting him to make up for their loss, to hell with them. It was their money he enjoyed the most; the feel of the new suits he bought with their grieving dimes. Ryan would put on the act of the concerned person, the one who wanted to help while deep inside he wanted nothing more than for them to join their loved ones.

Ryan finished the make-up on the dead woman and stood back. It seemed okay. He didn't really smooth out anything, but mostly packed on the make-up. The woman looked more like a clown than the classy pianist she was supposed to be. He grinned. They would accept anything he did for them. He was the Master.

He turned around to walk to the sink to wash his hands; of all times he had forgotten to wear his gloves. He cursed as the water hit his manicured hands.

"Not nice to swear young man."

Ryan turned quickly dropping the bar of soap on the floor. He rubbed his eyes.

"What the…" Ryan took a step back.

"What's wrong, you never seen a dead body before? I thought you worked here?" The woman smiled a somewhat toothless grin.

Ryan knew in the past few days sleep was something of a pastime. He knew he must have been seeing things. The woman sat up, parts of her were not fully attached, and while others were so half her body went lopsided. An arm barely hung on to her body. It swayed as she started to get up. The accident she was in severed many parts of her body. Ryan had thought his assistant had put together any parts that were torn apart. He reminded himself in his current state of fear to yell at his assistant.

"I know what you're thinking," the dead woman said as she moved closer to him. Ryan stepped back further and tried to maintain his balance.

"You're dead," Ryan whispered.

"Am I?" The woman laughed. She inched closer to Ryan, arms looking as if she was flying, they were flapping so much.

Ryan didn't understand. He saw the woman dead on the table. He just had finished her make-up.

"What do you want from me?" Ryan had now pinned himself against the large door behind him.

"Don't you know young man?"

Ryan's eyes widened. Of all days for him to miss a date with Jerry, to come here and make sure she was done and now this.

"Don't you like me?" The woman took one of her half attached arms and tried to rub down her other arm, showing Ryan what she was like.

He watched as she moved closer. Her body becoming decomposed right in front of her and confusion set in. He couldn't figure out how she was decomposing so quickly.

It was impossible. He had prepared so many dead bodies before. How could one be messed up like this or better yet, how is it that she is moving?

"I don't understand what you want from me." Ryan started shaking.

"My dear, you should know. I've heard you."

Ryan looked around. "Heard what?"

"Your thoughts."

Ryan swallowed hard. He could feel everything he had eaten for that snack starting to come up.

"I don't know what you mean," Ryan said slowly.

"All you want is money for us, don't you?" The woman almost slid across the floor. Her feet dragged behind her in a most distorted way. Ryan shook his head no.

"Now, now, is it nice to lie to your elders?" She was almost to where Ryan was standing. He turned quickly to open the door, but it was jammed. He tried jerking it free. It wouldn't budge.

Ryan turned back slightly to see the woman still approaching.

"Why me!" He screamed.

"Why you? You're the one that takes our lives, turns them around and for what, so that you can kill us later to retrieve your money?" The woman's eyes dead from all life looked hollow and black with anger.

"No, I give you your life back. I give your loved ones a sense of comfort," Ryan pleaded.

"And how much does this comfort cost?" The woman spoke and lost a couple of her decomposed teeth. Her eyes started to fill with ooze that dripped partially down her cheeks. Ryan gagged.

Ryan could feel his heart racing. He looked over to his right as he saw three more corpses stumbling toward him. The two men and one woman were decomposed beyond recognition; maggots had buried themselves in any opening on the dead peoples' body. Ryan screamed. He turned around; facing the door he started pounding with his fists.

"Let me out!" He had hoped his assistant was still there. She should still be on her shift; yet still there was no one that answered the door.

The woman and three other corpses were right at Ryan. He turned just in time to see all four starting attacking him. They tore at his plastic jacket, ripping it apart. They started chewing at his flesh, ripping it a part into pieces. The old woman pushed her hand into Ryan's chest, blood spurted everywhere and Ryan slid to the floor.·

#

Lina unlocked the door into the preparation room. As the door opened it pushed against Ryan's dead body. She looked down at his corpse and smiled. The four dead people who had chewed away at his body were gone. The window in back was smashed where they had made their exit into the world of the living.

Lina set down a brown folder that she was carrying under her arm and opened it. Inside contained paperwork and journal entries that Ryan had filled out. The papers told of how each client was searched out, killed and their families contacted for funeral arrangements. Ryan had personally killed these people to make more money off of them than he could possibly imagine. He had made his mistake when the first victim happened to be Lina's sister who had changed her name after she had gotten married. Ryan never knew that because Lina was hired only five days prior.

Lina was happy that Ryan had allowed her to embalm these particular corpses. It was only the second day she was working she had found this folder and saw her sister's picture. She had vowed revenge with the new formula she had made that came from her friends that visited the funeral home and also dabbled in death and magic. It turned out perfectly. The dead would rise again and take care of people like Ryan and perhaps just people in general. She had always hated people.

She closed up the folder and looked at Ryan's torn body. It pleased her to think finally her sister could be revenged. Lina took the folder off the table and threw it on the floor next to Ryan. If anyone would come into this place ever again they would find him with the folder. She would only hope that he would just rot in this room like those rotting corpses that are now among the living.

Turnpike

Darkness came quickly. Shadows trickled onto the sidewalk as if the sun never went down, so bold that the naked eye could see them. They flew past houses made of brick, old, traditional style houses from the 1940's. One house at a time they flew by waiting for the next person to die.

The shadows' faces were dark and not seen easily. Yet, faces made-up of all the souls they took. One by one, the souls swirled in the faces, screaming with fear, but trapped forever. Each night these shadows circled the small town of Haversville.

***

Sara, a journalist from a neighboring city came to Haversville to investigate the disappearances of several residents that occurred in the past two months. The town seemed quite, like nothing had recently happened. She parked her old escort in front of the General Grocery Store. Getting out, her hand brushed past her forehead, sweat dripping down. The weather in Haversville was hot.

She opened the door that creaked loudly. An older man dressed in overalls and a plaid shirt greeted her as she walked in.

"Hello, can I help you?" His voice sounded friendly enough to Sara and she smiled.

"Hi, I was just here to…" She stopped herself thinking that a small town might not be too welcoming to a stranger from a newspaper investigating their town.

"Yes?" The man said confused.

"I was stopping through, am pretty new to this area and was wondering if you could tell me the closest hotel?"

"We don't have hotels here." He looked at her. His eyes fierce, yet somehow a friendly sparkle remained.

"Oh, I'm sorry I had no idea." She looked around the store.

"We do have a small inn located four miles south of the store here. I'm sure Margie would love to have new visitors."

"Four miles south you say?" She looked outside at the clouds that were starting to turn black.

"I'd say miss, you may want to get a going. Storms here are not easy to drive in." Sara nodded. She turned once again to thank the man and headed back to her car. Looking up she saw the clouds moving quicker. Quickly she turned the key in the ignition and headed to the inn.

The inn seemed deserted. Shutters were falling off the windows and the grass was long. She parked her car on the gravel lot. Getting out she looked at the old building.

"Up keep must be really good here," she said to herself softly. Walking up to the old wooden door, she turned the rusty knob and walked in. Stairs were leading to an upstairs where rooms were located for guests. An old woman who wore a dress torn on the bottom walked slowly from the corner room and up to the front desk.

"We don't like strangers in our town."

"I'm sorry I was just passing through and needed a place to stay." The woman scowled, said something under her breath and stared at Sara.

"If it's for one night, fine, but you leave this town soon after. You hear me?"

"Um, sure, I understand." Sara frowned. The woman gave her an old brass key with the number six on it and pointed upstairs. Sara nodded and carefully stepped on the broken stairs. The hallway was dusty and brown. She looked around at the other doors that were smoke stained, turned around and unlocked her door.

Inside a broken wooden chair and an old desk, a bed, was all she saw. She threw down her purse on the desk and sat down on the bed. Pushing down with her hand, she felt the rock-hardness of an old mattress. Sara sighed. She looked at the window curtains that were brown and lacey. Not what she was use to staying in, but things with this town didn't seem normal anyways.

The wind howled at the window, which startled and caused her to stare out the pane glass. She got up and moved closer to the window to look out at the storm. A shadow blazed by the window. Sara blinked her eyes.

She thought she saw something but she wasn't sure. Pulling back the curtains, she tried to look outside more. All she saw was darkness, clouds moving fast, and droplets of rain hitting the window.

The shadow hovered right above where the window started. Sara thought about opening the window to check closer, but the storm was getting worse. She stood back and thought some more. The journalist in her wanted to know what was out there. Moving forward to the window, she opened it. The howling of the wind and the rain brushed past her face and soaked her hair. She looked down outside.

Being only on the second floor, she could easily jump out to the ground. Pushing through the window, she fell to the ground with a thud. She wiped her pants off and stood up. Sara looked around, unknown to her that the shadow lurked right above her. A rotten smell came to her nose and she shook her head to try to avoid it. She looked up and saw something black, but could not make it out fully because of the hard rain.

The shadow made a gurgling noise. A noise Sara heard. Fear grasped her breath and for a split moment, she thought she would die. She ran, ran as fast as possible past the inn to her car. If nothing else she could drive out of this town and forget she was ever here. The ground was wet from the rain making it slippery. She fell several times trying to slosh her way through the grass. The shadow flew overhead, never lowering itself, but always just above her.

The sound never left it. As she ran, all she could hear was that constant gurgling, signaling the approach of whatever that thing was. Finally, she got to her car, stepped in and tried the key in the ignition. The car tried but did not turn over.

"Come on!" She yelled, but nothing happened. The shadow hovered above her front windshield. She looked up and saw its face. All the souls swirled deep within its black cover. Sara screamed, but sat frozen at the shock of it. The shadow gurgled again, but did not move forward at her. She gathered herself and just tried to make out its face. Still scared, she tried to move forward without shaking this thing up.

The shadow with all its souls stood staring back, flying still above her windshield. She hesitated, but opened her car door and got out. The shadow flew right to her face. Sara gasped and stood frozen in fear. As the shadow was right by her face, it stopped its gurgling and just stared at her.

Sara looked back and then with all she could muster yelled at it.

"What is it you want!?"

The shadow said nothing at first and than instead of a gurgling noise it spoke.

"I am but one of many." The voice was deep and echoic.

"One of what many?" She asked.

"Many of those that shall pay." Sara stared at the faces of those that were lost, souls taken by this particular shadow.

"Who will pay?"

"This place, these humans."

"Why?"

"They cause death."

"Who caused death?" The shadow posed one of its shadowy fingers in the right direction. Sara followed its hand. Where the shadow pointed was the turnpike. Trees swayed back and forth from the storm. She was hardly able to make out anything there. Yet, she followed where the shadow had pointed. Walking, she pushed her bangs from her forehead. Soaked, she kept walking toward the road.

She stopped when she saw more of the creatures like the one that talked to her. They were flying around the turnpike, swarming like locusts. Sara walked further, closer to where the rest of the shadows were. The gurgling noise was loud. Many shadows hovered above the road staring down at her. She looked up. Taking a deep breath, she continued on, but fell a pull on her leg.

Sara screamed and tried to pull her leg from whatever was holding it. She looked down at a rotted hand grabbing on to her ankle, trying to pull her underneath the road. Pulling seemed no use and Sara fell onto the street's surface. The hand dragged her and she started to feel the street surrounding her body. Her screams becoming muffled from strain.

The shadows kept flying overhead, watching as the hand pulled Sara further and further down. She clawed at the top of the asphalt that now surrounded her chest. Fingernails digging

into the surface, bleeding, chipping, as she struggled to maintain some kind of hold. She started to slip further down when something suddenly grabbed her hand and started pulling her back up. Startled, but in a sense relieved, she didn't fight it.

Finally pulled back up to the surface, she stood shaking, trying to regain her composure. A man stood in front of her, cloaked in black with a strange wide brimmed hat, eyes dark, yet visible. Sara stood staring at him, trying to speak, but the man spoke first.

"You should not be here. You are not from here."

"I... Well, I..." He gestured up to the shadows flying overhead and they flew away from the road.

"This road, this turnpike is not for you."

"Then who?" Her voice and body still shaking.

"For them." He pointed back to the town. Sara looked back.

"Why?"

"They cause death, death takes them back." She stood confused, shocked and frozen in place with fear.

"Caused death?" She repeated the question as if he never said anything.

"Killed little ones, here, this road."

"Killed, you mean children?" He nodded and pointed down at the road's surface. She stood looking down at the road.

"Death took them because of them. They were not ready for death. Death did not want them yet."

"But how, how did they kill them?"

"Through play, through grass, building. It became death."

"Play, was this a playground before, or where children played?" He nodded again.

"Poison, black cloud, destroyed little ones." He looked down.

"Poison, chemicals?" She asked, but was also thinking out loud.

"Poison, yes, little ones die."

She remembered in her research about this town that a chemical plant was a big business for a while, shut down for undisclosed reasons. Given the situation, she didn't have her map with her. Thinking to herself and more calmed than she was, the chemical plant was probably located right by this road, except at the time it was not a road, but maybe a park.

"The road was built over the play area?" The man nodded yes. Her eyes widened in shock. The town had built a road over the play area to cover the evidence. The people that were disappearing, from what she had read, were people that were here during the time. Those people disappearing because of what happened with the plant and the children.

"Little ones down below." Once again he pointed to the street. She looked down. The children must have been buried here.

"Buried here, graves here?" She asked. The man shook his head no.

"How can…how can they be down there ?" A thought came to her just as she asked that. "They were just covered over?" She stood back from the man. The shock of what she just thought made her loose her balance. The man looked up and nodded yes.

"All this time, children under here, dead and the town knew this and did this?" The man nodded again.

"You must leave, this is not for you. You know now, must go." Sara nodded, but asked one final question.

"But, who are you, why do you stay?"

"I am Death's keeper. I am here for little one's. I help give back life."

"By taking the people from this town?" He nodded.

"Leave, now, this not for you." He pointed to the city close by. "Go there, that is for you." She looked at the nearby city, walking it would take her two hours. Sara looked at the man once more and nodded. She started to walk slowly, making sure the man or the shadows would not follow. Cautiously, she looked back. The man was no longer there and the shadows had disappeared.

***

Several days later Sara was sitting at a local dinner and reading the newspaper. After the incident at Haversville, she had quit her job as an investigative reporter. The rumors still flew about that town located in the middle of nowhere, people still missing and never found. She knew she would never return to that place, that town or to that turnpike. Drinking her cup of coffee, she happened to glance up. A man wearing a black overcoat and a wide brimmed hat noticed her and tipped his hat forward in acknowledgement. He was gone in an instant.

Tooth Decay

Turn me off now and I would be happy. I can't stop myself from the taste. It engrosses me and fills me. Each night it becomes the same. I chase, they run and I eat. Feelings of compassion have all left this old wearing shell I used to call a body.

My skin, if you want to call it that, is pale and blue. Death does that to a person. And at one time I used to be a person. When that changed I became something that one thinks of in the night, one that is feared but not seen. Every night I walk these streets, not seen by anything or anyone except my own kind.

There is competition out there when it comes for food. One would think being a vampire there wouldn't be. The world isn't what I had remembered. It has changed. Humans are not in vast supply. The plague has taken them and also taken most of my food source. They have now become the undead, walking around searching for people to populate into what they are.

There are only a few of my kind left now because of the undead. Slowly we are being exterminated because of lack of food. They bite at whatever is there and so do we. Their population is growing by the hundreds each day, while ours is slowly withering away to nothing.

I hear more screams in the night than I remembered. My kind is pretty discrete when it comes to killing. No one knows where we are even when feasting occurs. The undead are not as discrete. As they walk in their rotten skins with worms dripping out of every hole that was created, people run and then they scream. I stand in the shadows of a building every night watching people run past me into their final doom.

My kind doesn't talk to one another; if we did we might be able to solve the problem of the undead taking all our meat. I have tried conversing with another of my kind one day. I was shrugged off and almost pushed out of the way as he tried to run after a human that had a horde of undead after them already.

***

Standing here behind the usual building I did every night, I watched hundreds of them walk, crawl and slide past me. I smell for human blood, but smell nothing; the taste of it now only familiar to memories of past feastings. If I venture outside of my building, it is only to scatter amongst the puss and smell of the undead pushing past me for another human.

I will try it anyways tonight. My claws that use to be fingernails scrap across the bricks of the building. The undead are flocking around a window of the building. There must be a human hiding in there. Sliding across the side of the building, my sight keener than ever, I spot a blonde haired woman crouched below a wooden desk. The undead are trying to push the windows and door open, but are unable to.

If I move just so I should be able to get through the window without breaking it. If I did break it, the undead would surely pass through to get the woman and I would be without food again. I had to make sure that even in my hunger state that no mistakes were made. My continued sliding across the wall did not draw attention from the undead still trying to push against the windows or door.

I made it to the front of the door. The breath of these undead creatures is making me ill. They are such disgusting creatures. The puss is just drooling out of their eye sockets. I am about to gag. But my focus needs to remain on the woman. I should jump through the window, but if the glass broke, the undead would surely follow. The choice is not mine. I need food, blood to survive; this is the only way.

My claws pushed against the window. I heard a small snap as the glass was breaking. The undead looked at my breakage and stood there. I was certain they would start to push harder at the window now. They weren't that smart and continued to stand there. The glass cut my arms, but healed right away as I made my way in. The woman shaking didn't notice I was present.

The quickness I once had was not the same anymore. I barely made it over to her. The weakness from not feasting for days is starting to take its toll. The woman was crouched into a ball underneath the wooden desk. A desk I remembered having once in my life time. A time that was different from now.

I slide underneath the desk, still not noticed. The woman brought up her head and darted her eyes back and forth. I am assuming it was to look for undead creatures coming her way. Her arm I went to touch, but she pulled away not noticing how close I was to her now. My fangs starting pushing past the gums I once knew as human parts. Sharp as they still were I only hoped my energy would prevail and I would be able to feast again at last.

The screaming started as soon as my fangs pinched and then drove into her skin. I felt her heart panic from fear of the unknown hurting her. The blood was raw, was fresh of the young woman. It felt wonderful to be able to feast again. I was almost finished when the undead managed to break through the small crack I had started in the window.

Some were starting to have their face literally drip down from what used to be their human skulls. I was not willing to give up this woman. She was mine. I stood my ground. They had no idea I was before them. All they smelled was a human not yet converted into their type of disgusting being. I clawed at one that approached the woman.

He made a growl. My nails were now covered with the goop they use to call flesh. I tossed the skin pieces to the floor and gagged. Nothing was viler than having any parts of them near me.

They kept coming. Hordes of them pushed through the glass until finally there was a large opening enough for all of them. I started dragging the woman to the other room, my strength still not strong enough to fly away with her. I locked the door behind me. The pounding against the door started immediately and I knew they would keep going until they could no longer smell the woman, stupid creatures.

I looked at the woman who was barely breathing now. The door would hold for only a few moments yet. I might as well finish the woman. My fangs once again punctured her skin. Blood flowed easily into me and the taste once again refreshing. Soon afterward she was dead. I licked my lips and my fangs retracted. The pounding subsided. They smelled the woman's now dead body and figured it was one of them, stupid creatures.

I dropped the woman's limp body to the floor and stood up. Most of my strength, at least temporally was back. I made a choice in the very instant to go outside. Pushing my way past the hundreds of undead that loaded the street, I made my way to the park. A lot of my kind seemed to hover in that area. Passing by me a few humans ran and a few undead slowly crept up to them. I was full now and didn't care what happened to the pathetic humans.

The undead made progress on the humans and the biting of the flesh continued. I was watching as their body parts became part of their ritual. Parts now were on the ground scattered and soon the humans would become part of the undead. I turned as I heard a growl to my left. Another one of my kind was angry at the undead and went full force at the ten now feasting on the man lying on the ground.

I kept watching out of amusement more or less. I knew that someday my kind would be no more. The humans stupid in their ways over populated this world and created a plague that would destroy them and anything left. Soon there would be nothing but the undead roaming the streets, in buildings and anywhere they could crawl into.

I pitied the vampire who was attacking ten of them now. He would be no match for their killing skills. Even undetected he would be pushed into the horde and soon munched on for something to do. They would not see him or smell him, but they might be able to feel him next to the human who was still alive. We smell differently when we are hungry next to a fresh human.

I put my hands above my head and watched as one more of my kind got eaten by the undead. He would be lucky not to turn into one of them. I laughed for awhile and knew I would be back to competing for a dying food source. The undead would win and soon I would be no more, along with the rest of my kind.

About the Author

Shells Walter has been writing since she was young. Her book *Dead Practices* was a Top Ten finisher in the *Predators and Editors Poll*.

She currently writes in every genre and format. Her favorite still remains Horror stories.

Shells lives in the South-Eastern part of the U.S. with her husband, two girls and five cats.

You can find out more about Shells and contact her at:
www.shellswalter.com

www.ingramcontent.com/pod-product-compliance
Lightning Source LLC
Chambersburg PA
CBHW022132170626
46808CB00002B/959